"How incredibly pompous you sound, Tritia!

"I'm going back to work, too, you know, and living in a country house is no new thing for Philomena. Her own home is a charming one in England with surroundings just as lovely as these."

He kissed his mother, waved to Tritia and shook his head at her as he opened the car door for Philomena. But he didn't mention Tritia's rudeness during the short drive, instead talking about nothing much until they arrived at Mevrouw de Winter's door, where he stood quietly while Philomena thanked him for her weekend.

He looked down at her, smiling a little. "It was rather spoilt, wasn't it? We must make up for it next time."

She had the sad thought that there was unlikely to be a next time. Tritia would see to that, and perhaps it would be as well—her suddenly surprised mind warned her that falling in love with one's rich, handsome employer was something which happened in novels, not to real girls such as herself.

Romance readers around the world were sad to note the passing of **Betty Neels** in June 2001. Her career spanned thirty years, and she continued to write into her ninetieth year. To her millions of fans, Betty epitomized the romance writer, and yet she began writing almost by accident. She had retired from nursing, but her inquiring mind still sought stimulation. Her new career was born when she heard a lady in her local library bemoaning the lack of good romance novels. Betty's first book, *Sister Peters in Amsterdam,* was published in 1969, and she eventually completed 134 books. Her novels offer a reassuring warmth that was very much a part of her own personality. She was a wonderful writer, and she will be greatly missed. Her spirit and genuine talent will live on in all her stories.

THE BEST *of*

BETTY NEELS

PHILOMENA'S MIRACLE

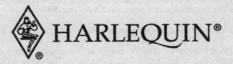

HARLEQUIN®

TORONTO • NEW YORK • LONDON
AMSTERDAM • PARIS • SYDNEY • HAMBURG
STOCKHOLM • ATHENS • TOKYO • MILAN • MADRID
PRAGUE • WARSAW • BUDAPEST • AUCKLAND

ISBN-13: 978-0-373-19885-6
ISBN-10: 0-373-19885-X

PHILOMENA'S MIRACLE

CHAPTER ONE

THE CORRIDOR was long and austere, its walls coloured a dreary margarine, its paintwork brown varnished, the floor a shiny lino, cracked here and there, the whole very clean and uninviting despite the early April sunlight streaming through its long, narrow windows along one side. But to Nurse Philomena Parsons it was fairyland; the whole world was fairyland, for in her pocket was the letter informing her that she had been placed on the State Register; she had passed her finals, she could wear a silver buckle on her belt now and the world was her oyster. If it hadn't been for the fact that Commander Frost, RN retired, whom she was wheeling to X-Ray in a chair, was in one of his nasty tempers, she might have broken into a gay whistle or danced a few steps as she pushed, but the old gentleman was in a crusty mood that morning and although she was so happy herself she had a soft heart which sympathised with his jaundiced outlook on life; probably, she conceded, at his age and in his circumstances, she would be crusty too, so she agreed with his mutterings about the inconvenience of being taken to X-Ray at eight o'clock in the morning in a low gentle voice which did much to soothe his feelings, smiling to herself as she spoke, thinking of the letter in her pocket. The smile was a charming one, lighting her mediocre features to prettiness and bringing a sparkle to her lovely green eyes, fringed with preposterously long lashes; her one beauty, unless one counted the honey-gold hair, long and thick and fine and pulled back into such a severe bun that its beauty, for the most part, was lost.

It would be necessary to take a lift down to X-Ray; there were two halfway down the corridor and she could see that there was someone waiting by them. The lifts were old and shaky and no one other than patients and their attendant nurses or porters was allowed to use them. The man waiting didn't appear to come into any of these categories; he was leaning against the wall, his hands in his pockets, his eyes closed. He was very good-looking, Philomena considered, and very large; even when she unconsciously drew up her five feet three of nicely rounded person, she still had to look a long way up to him. She brought the chair to a smart halt in front of the lift and fell to studying him; good shoes, beautifully polished, a tweed suit which wasn't new but of a masterly cut, a sober tie…blue eyes were staring at her, so she said good morning politely.

'Good morning—and should there not be a porter to push that thing?' he asked.

She smiled at him. 'Oh, usually there is, but the porters are on an hour's strike about something or other.' She hesitated and added: 'Perhaps you don't know, but they're awfully fussy about anyone but patients and nurses using the lifts; they don't work very well, you see, and if they get overloaded they break down.'

For a moment he looked as though he was going to laugh, but his deep rather slow voice was quite serious. 'Kind of you to tell me, but don't you think that I should come with you in the lift to give a hand with that chair?'

The lift had arrived, making a dim, drumming sound as it settled in a wobbly way, and a very tall nurse carrying a small girl got out. Her 'Hi, Philly, congrats,' was called over her shoulder as she swept past them, and as the man manoeuvred the wheelchair into the lift he asked in an interested voice: 'Getting married or engaged or something of that sort?'

He set the chair just so, smiled at its occupant and then looked at Philomena, closing the doors. 'Me? Gracious, no.' The smile she couldn't suppress burst out again. 'I've passed my finals—I've just heard.'

His congratulations were sincere as he pressed the button and their unsteady conveyance began lurching downwards. 'Cause for celebration,' he added kindly.

The smile faded just a little. 'Well, I don't expect I shall—I—don't go home very often, it's rather a long way away, and the other girls who passed have all got someone—family or boy-friends...'

His eyes were very kind. 'Hard luck, but very exciting, all the same.'

The lift wobbled and stopped and Commander Frost, deep in his own thoughts, said suddenly: 'She puts me in mind of my dear Lucy—listens when I say something and then gives me an intelligent answer—not pretty, of course.' He gave Philomena a surprisingly intelligent look. 'You'll make a good wife, my dear.'

Philomena blushed, a regrettable shortcoming which she had never been able to overcome. 'Thank you, Commander.' She was pulling back the doors as she spoke and didn't look at either of her companions. The big man wheeled the patient out of the lift and into the passage for her and got back into the lift. 'You really oughtn't to,' pointed out Philomena. 'Supposing you get caught?' She added: 'Thank you for your help.'

He smiled and began to close the lift doors. 'A pleasure.' The doors closed and he was away again. Philomena sighed gently; she would have liked to see more of him, he looked nice and he had been friendly and helpful. Probably he was going to the Private Wing to see one of the patients; she decided to forget him.

'He would make you a splendid husband,' observed the Commander, à propos nothing at all.

The morning was busy, but it had its moments; Philomena was bidden to the Principal Nursing

Officer's office, congratulated, informed that she was the Gold Medallist for her year and it was intimated by Miss Blake that when a vacancy for a Ward Sister occurred, she would be invited to apply for it. She went back to her ward telling herself that she was the luckiest girl alive and went on telling herself so while she worked her way through the dressings to be done before dinners. Only she wasn't quite the luckiest, she admitted, allowing the thoughts she kept tucked away at the back of her head to air themselves for once; the luckiest girl would have a family to tell her how clever she was and how proud they were of her—moreover, she would have someone bearing a marked resemblance to the man in the lift waiting for her when she got off duty, eager to take her out and celebrate. She popped her thoughts back again where they belonged and turned an attentive ear to Mr Wilkinson's cheery Cockney voice while she deftly removed the stitches from the complicated wound which Mr Dale, the consultant surgeon, had so meticulously stitched together.

'Going out to celebrate, Staff?' Mr Wilkinson wanted to know. 'Live in Wareham, don't you? Family coming up to make a night of it?'

She snipped a particularly complicated piece of Mr Dale's needlework. 'It's a bit too far.' She made her voice cheerful. 'And my stepmother hates driving long distances…'

'No sisters or brothers?' he asked sympathetically.

'Oh, yes—two stepsisters.' Both of them excellent drivers, both owning their own cars, neither of them caring twopence whether she passed her exams or not, not because they disliked her, it was just that they had nothing in common. Both they and her stepmother gave her a tolerant affection which stopped short at putting themselves out in any way for her. They had never put themselves out for anyone, although they had loved her father, not very deeply but with charming demonstration so that Philomena, who found it difficult to be deliberately charming, appeared reserved towards him, and yet, when he had died a year or two previously, her sorrow had been deep and genuine whereas they had quickly adjusted to life without him in the pleasant roomy old house on the outskirts of Wareham.

They had been well provided for and neither they nor her stepmother had been able to understand why Philomena hadn't left nursing at once and adopted the pleasant leisurely life they led. But she hadn't wanted to do that; she loved her home, but she loved nursing too, so she had stayed at Faith's, making a successful career for herself and happy too, for she was well liked and had a great number of friends. She went home, of course, and her stepmother and Miriam and Chloe welcomed her affectionately, but they never asked her about her work; hospitals smacked to them of the more unpleasant side of life. They arranged a party or two for her, took her with them when they went riding or

driving to visit friends, and then after a day or two took
it for granted that they had done their share of entertain-
ing her and drifted off with their own particular friends
again, leaving her quite happily to garden or drive
herself around in the little Mini her father had given her
when she had had her twenty-first birthday. And if she
felt lonely she never admitted it, even to herself.

She removed the last stitch, sprayed the scar, said
'There, as good as new, Mr Wilkinson,' collected up her
instruments, and nipped down the ward, just in time to
help Sister Brice with the dinners. The ward was full with
not an empty bed in it, and that afternoon there would be
several cases for theatre. Philomena, spooning potatoes
on to the plates with the expertise of long practice, reflected that she would be lucky to get off at five o'clock.
Not that it would matter, she wasn't going anywhere.

The afternoon was even busier than she had antici-
pated. The first case for theatre turned out to be a
leaking abdominal aneurysm, which had presented
symptoms very similar to an appendix and needed a
good deal more surgery; the patient returned from the
recovery room an hour later than she had expected,
consequently the other three patients were all tardy too,
and over and above that two beds had to be put up down
the centre of the ward to accommodate street accidents.
Five o'clock came and with it Sister Brice, but there was
no hope of getting off duty; it was almost an hour later
when she finally gave her report and started on her way

to the changing room, and before she reached it, Potter, the Head Porter, stopped her to tell her that she was wanted in the front hall.

For a moment she hoped that it was her stepmother or her sisters, a hope to be dismissed immediately as nonsense; they had never been near the hospital, and besides, they didn't know that she had had her results that morning. It could be one of her friends from Wareham, in London for a visit and calling on the offchance of seeing her—taking her out, perhaps. She pushed her cap back a little impatiently on her still neat head and retraced her footsteps. Old Mrs Fox, perhaps, who had been a friend of her mother's years ago, or Mary Burns, in town to shop, or that boring Tim Crooks... She whisked round the last corner and saw that it was none of these people, so she stopped and looked around her, for the only person there was the man she had met in the lift that morning, lounging against the window of the porter's lodge, apparently asleep. But he wasn't; he straightened up and came towards her, and when she said uncertainly: 'Hullo—have you seen anyone...'

'Not a soul,' he assured her blandly, 'I'm the only one here.'

'Oh—I expect it was a mistake; Potter said that someone wanted to see me.'

'Correct, I do.'

She raised bewildered green eyes to his and asked simply: 'Why?'

He smiled very nicely. 'I wondered if you would take pity on me and come out to dinner—unless you have other plans.'

'No, I haven't.' She added cautiously: 'I don't know your name…'

'Walle van der Tacx.'

'Oh, Dutch, are you not?' She held out a hand and he shook it gravely. 'I stayed in Amsterdam for a few days with my father…'

'I'm afraid I can't claim to live there, my home is a mile or so from a small town called Ommen, twenty kilometres or so to the east of Zwolle and roughly a hundred and thirty from Amsterdam. I have a country practice there.'

'Oh, you're a doctor!' The relief in her voice caused his firm mouth to twitch. 'Well then, I'd like to come very much—but haven't you anything better to do?'

The twitch came and went, but his blue eyes were kind. 'I can think of nothing better. I'm hungry and I hope you are too; dining alone can be extremely dull.'

'Haven't you any friends here?'

'Several, but none of them free this evening.' His voice was casual and she believed him. 'Shall we meet here in half an hour? We might try one of those restaurants in Soho.'

Philomena was halfway across the hall when she turned back. 'Why me?' she asked.

'We did meet this morning,' he reminded her.

'Besides, you have a good reason to celebrate, haven't you, and I hoped that would decide you to come.'

Such a sensible answer that she agreed happily.

The Nurses' Home was noisy; a dozen or more of its inmates had passed their exams too and all of them were going out with boy-friends, fiancés or family. Philomena had her head in her cupboard, deciding what she would wear, when Jenny Pringle, one of her closer friends, drifted in with a mug of tea. Her hair was in rollers and her face heavily creamed in preparation for the evening's festivities, but she put the mug down on the dressing table and sat herself down on the bed, prepared to gossip for a few minutes.

'What are you doing, Philly?' she asked cautiously, mindful of the fact that Philomena was probably not doing anything exciting like the rest of them.

'Finding something to wear.' Philomena's muffled voice came from the depths of the cupboard, but she emerged a few moments later. 'Tea,' she exclaimed, 'how nice. Do I look my poor best in this pink thing or the green?'

'You're going out!' Jenny was genuinely delighted; they all liked Philly and most of them knew that her home life wasn't as happy as it might have been, and besides, she hadn't a boy-friend; she got taken out occasionally by one or other of the housemen, but sooner or later their eyes were caught by someone a great deal prettier than she was. 'Who with?'

'Doctor Walle van der Tacx.'

'You're joking!' Jenny kicked off her slippers and tucked her feet under her. 'A name like that!'

'He's Dutch.' Philomena had decided on the green, nicely cut, simple and just right for her eyes. 'I met him today in a lift, he's hungry and doesn't like eating his dinner alone, so he asked me if I'd go with him.'

Her friend looked at her in utter astonishment; it was so unlike Philly to go on a blind date. Of course she had been knocked off balance by reason of the final results, but even so, it didn't seem like her at all.

'Is he nice?' asked Jenny anxiously.

'I think so.' Philomena added, 'He lives at a place called Ommen,' as though that proved that his credentials were beyond doubt. 'Shall I wear my hair up or down?'

'Down—you always look so severe with it piled up like that, and it's pretty hair.'

'I don't think he'll notice.' Philomena was tearing out of her clothes, pausing to gulp tea as she did so. 'There'd better be a bathroom free, he said half an hour.'

'Where are you going to meet?'

'The front hall.' Philomena had snatched up a towel and was making for the bathroom. 'He said something about Soho…' She pattered away, unheeding of her friend's: 'But you don't really know him!'

She was ready with five minutes to spare and as it hadn't entered her head to keep him waiting, she went down to the front hall. He was waiting for her, leaning up against the Porter's Lodge again, deep in conversation with Potter. He came to meet her at once with a cheerful: 'There you are—punctual too, a rare thing in a woman.'

She was too shy to ask how he was so sure of this, and anyway there was no need for her to say anything much, for he swept her out of the main entrance on a steady gentle flow of small talk which saw them safely into the car standing in the forecourt, but on the point of getting in she stopped short. 'A Maserati—one of the new ones—a Khamsin.' She had stopped to look at one in a car showroom only a few days previously and had been shocked to see its price—almost eighteen thousand pounds! One could buy a house for that, or live comfortably for four or five years.

Her companion opened the door a little wider. 'Easy to get around in,' he told her in a placid matter-of-fact voice which made its price seem quite reasonable after all.

'Do you travel a great deal?' she asked him as he got in beside her.

'Quite frequently—I have a sister living in the south of France.' He swung the car neatly into the evening traffic. 'Do you drive?'

She told him about the Mini. 'I keep it at home, though, I'm not much good in London traffic.'

'No? But surely it would be useful when you go home?'

Philomena looked out of the window, not really seeing the cars streaming along in the clear April evening. 'I don't go very often.'

He didn't question her further but embarked on the kind of conversation which needed little reply on her part, but which nonetheless put her at her ease. 'You said Soho,' she reminded him presently as he turned up into Shaftesbury Avenue. 'I've never been there—not for a meal, I mean.'

'I thought we might go to Kettner's.' He had turned the car into Frith Street and then into Romilly Street and they had stopped before she could say anything. She had heard of the restaurant, of course, but the few evenings out she had enjoyed had ended at more homely places; young doctors tended to choose a steak bar or the Golden Egg, but this was something different; she was heartily glad that she had worn the green dress and taken pains with her face and hair.

They were shown to a table at once—presumably he had booked one while she was changing—and she sat back and looked around her with unconcealed pleasure. 'What a super place!' Her wide mouth curved in a lovely smile. 'You're very kind to bring me here.'

'It is you who are kind to keep me company—and may I call you Philomena?' He lifted a finger to the hovering waiter. 'I shan't ask you what you would like to drink—we'll celebrate with champagne.'

And probably it was the champagne which gave

Philomena the pleasant feeling that Doctor van der Tacx
was an old friend, and when presently he suggested
mildly that she might call him Walle, she agreed readily
enough before getting down to the serious business of
deciding what they should eat. In the end she took his
advice, given in a casual almost unnoticed way, and
chose paté maison, a magnificent dish of lobster, fried
with herbs and then covered and set alight with cognac,
and rounded these delights off with Vacherin.

'That was sheer heaven,' she assured her host over
coffee, 'I've never had such a gorgeous meal and in such
a super place.' She beamed at him widely. 'I never
thought I'd celebrate like this.'

He smiled back at her. 'Perhaps you will have your
celebrations next time you go home,' and when she
didn't answer: 'You live a long way away?'

A hundred and thirteen miles was nothing; three
hours at the most and in a car such as his, much less; a
loving family or a devoted boy-friend would have made
light of it. She said reluctantly: 'Not so very—my
home's at Wareham, in Dorset.'

His only comment was: 'Ah, yes—a charming place,
I've been sailing in those parts,' and at her questioning
look, he added blandly: 'I was up at Cambridge for
some years and I have friends in England—I spent a
good deal of time with a fellow student who was mad
on sailing.' He laughed. 'Lord, it makes one feel old!'

She hadn't really thought about his age; his hair was

fair and thick and silvering at the temples, but he had the kind of good looks which would be very much as they were now in twenty years' time. 'You're not old,' said Philomena. 'I'm twenty-three.'

He dropped the heavy lids over his eyes to hide their sudden gleam of amusement. 'And I am thirty-six.'

'That's not in the least old. I expect you're at the height of your career and very content with your life and everything in the world to look forward to.'

'Thank you, Philomena. Until now I have been more than content with my life, but now I'm not so sure.' He gave her a thoughtful look. 'You know you haven't asked me if I'm married.'

The champagne had made her decidedly chatty. 'Well, no, but I don't think you are…'

'Do tell why?'

'Well, you're not the kind of man who would— would ask the first girl you met to go out to dinner with him if you were married.'

'You're right of course, but too flattering. I don't fancy that you know much about men.'

She poured more coffee. 'No, I don't. You see, I don't go out a great deal with them—there are so many pretty girls in hospital, and of course the housemen go for them first.' She gave him a rather appalled look; the champagne had certainly made ducks and drakes of her usual quiet matter-of-factness. If he paid her a compliment now about being pretty, she would hate him for it.

He didn't. He said with calm: 'Young men always go for the pretty girls, that's human nature, but young men grow up, you know.'

Probably he was right; he had a very assured way of speaking so that one believed him, and besides that, she felt at ease with him, as though they had been old friends for a very long time. She voiced her thoughts with unconscious forlornness. 'I suppose you'll be going back to Holland very soon?'

'No, I've several people to see over here and there's a seminar I'm going to in Edinburgh. I've two partners in the practice so that we can all get away now and again. I've promised to do some shopping for my mother and a cousin, perhaps you would help me with that? Tritia wanted to come with me, but she's only nineteen and what would I do with her while I'm at the hospital? And I certainly didn't want to take her to Edinburgh—she's pretty and spoilt, the kind of girl young men look at and then get to know without waste of time.'

Not like me, thought Philomena sadly. I expect he's in love with her. And to make it worse he added smoothly: 'She lives at my home for the moment, an aunt of mine whose adopted daughter she is, has gone to Canada to visit her son. I must say Tritia gives life an added zest.'

Philomena could see the girl vividly in her mind's eye; dazzlingly pretty, loaded with charm, small and dainty so that men rushed to open doors and lift things for her... Why, oh, why couldn't she have been just a little like that? Certainly she was small, but she was what her stepmother laughingly called verging on the plump, which somehow carried an awful warning of what she would be like in ten years' time, but prettiness had passed her by and she had always been in the habit of doing things for herself; no young man had ever felt the urge to open doors for her. She had charm, but she was quite unaware of that, just as she could see nothing remarkable about her green eyes and golden hair. She said humbly: 'She sounds quite something. I expect you like taking her out.'

He smiled at her across the table. 'Oh, I do, although I find it rather exhausting. She likes to dance until the small hours, on top of dinner too.' It was hardly the moment for him to ask Philomena if she would like to go on somewhere and dance.

She schooled her voice to polite regret and seethed under the green dress. 'I'm on early,' she explained in a slightly wooden voice. 'It's been a delightful evening and I've enjoyed it so much. I really should get back...'

He glanced at the paper-thin gold watch on his wrist. 'I did put it badly, didn't I? I'm sorry. Won't you change your mind? It's early—barely half past ten.'

And now he was being polite, which made it even worse—he must be thinking of that cousin and wishing she were opposite him now. Philomena stifled a strong urge to burst into tears for no reason at all and repeated, just as woodenly, her regrets.

He was too well mannered to persist. He said all the right things and asked for the bill and while he paid it she looked around her, making a note of her luxurious surroundings so that later, when her friends asked her where she had been, she would be able to give a glowing account of her evening. It had been a lovely evening, she chided herself silently, and why on earth should she expect a chance acquaintance who had been kind enough to ask her to share his dinner to be more than casually friendly? And kind. She mustn't forget that. She was aware, because her stepmother had told her so on many occasions, that she had very few social graces. It hadn't been said unkindly—her stepmother was too easy-going to be unkind—merely a stated fact; probably the doctor had been bored stiff for the entire evening...

'Why do you look so stricken?' asked her companion quietly.

Philomena composed her ordinary features into a smile. 'Oh, I suppose I was thinking about work tomorrow—rather a comedown after this.' She waved a small, practical and well-kept hand at their surroundings. 'An evening to remember—I can never thank you enough.' She added inconsequently: 'Celebrating after the occasion is never celebrating, is it?'

'No, Philomena, it isn't. Shall we go?'

The streets were quieter now and the short journey

seemed even shorter than it was. She couldn't remember afterwards what they talked about, but it couldn't have been anything important. He got out and opened the car door for her when they reached the hospital, and walked with her to the entrance. The old building loomed dark and almost silent around them, its small night noises almost unnoticed; the hiss of steam from the boiler room, a child's cry, the quiet voices coming from the Accident Room in the far corner and the bang of an ambulance door.

'Oh, well,' said Philomena, her hand on the door, and then took it away to offer to her companion. 'Thank you once again, Walle.' She smiled up at him, looming beside her in the dimness. 'I hope you enjoy your seminar.' She had quite forgotten the shopping.

His hand closed round hers. 'Goodnight, Philomena. I'm not much good at quoting, but your Shakespeare had the right words: "Fortune, goodnight, smile once more, turn thy wheel." *King Lear*, and rather apt, I would say.'

He opened the door for her and she went past him with a murmur. She longed to look back, but she didn't, hurrying through the hospital while his words rang in her ears. Had he been polite again, or had he meant it? Probably polite, she decided sensibly as she opened her room door, just to round off her evening for her.

She would have liked to have sat and thought about it, but there was no chance; several of her friends had returned from their own celebrations and someone had made the inevitable pot of tea; it was nice to be able to throw a careless 'Kettner's' at Jenny when she asked where she had been, and to see the looks of interest turned upon her person. Everyone broke into talk then, saying where they had been and what they had eaten, and just for once, instead of playing the role of interested listener, Philomena was able to toss back champagne, paté maison, lobster and Vacherin into the pool of conversation. She retired to bed presently, nicely sated with her companions' cries of 'Oh, Philly—how super!' She should have slept soundly in deep content, but she didn't; she lay awake for hours thinking about Doctor van der Tacx.

CHAPTER TWO

OF COURSE, Philomena overslept; she didn't doze off until the early hours of the morning and although she heard the night nurse's thump on her door, she turned right over and went to sleep again. The subdued thunder of nurses' feet and the banging of doors brought her awake again, and by dint of bundling her hair up anyway and doing nothing at all to her face, she managed to get down to the breakfast table in time to swallow a cup of tea and gobble bread and butter and marmalade before making for Men's Surgical. Sister had her days off, which made them short-handed for a start, and as well as that, there was a theatre list. Philomena took the report from the Night Staff Nurse, scanned the notes of the two new admissions since she had gone off duty, and plunged into the ward, to be instantly swallowed up in its routine. Drips to check, dressings to do, theatre preps, blood pressures—she didn't do them all, of course, but she had to check that they were being done. She was glad when she could escape to the office and drink her coffee, and even that precious five minutes was blighted by a telephone call from the second part-time staff nurse to say that her youngest had the measles and she wouldn't be coming in that afternoon. A sad blow for Philomena, for the other part-timer was on holiday, so it would mean that she would have to stay on duty all day and the next day as well, unless the Office sent someone to relieve her. But nobody suggested that when she telephoned the Office, only a harassed voice wanted to know if she thought she could manage. She replied that yes, she could and wondered fleetingly what would have been said if she had declared flatly that no, she couldn't.

The Registrar, Toby Brown, came in then, so that she had no time to feel sorry for herself; they did a round of the ward and she pointed out a little worriedly that Commander Frost didn't seem so well. He was naturally peppery, they both knew that, but now he seemed strangely subdued.

'Are the X-rays back?' asked Philomena. 'I wonder what they found? He's having trouble with his breathing…'

'The chief's got them—said he'd meet me here presently—they're not too good, I gather.' He gave her a brief glance. 'I say, Philly, you look like a wet week and I've quite forgotten to congratulate you—sorry. You deserved it, nice, hard-working girl that you are.'

She was digesting this sincere but not too flattering remark when Mr Dale arrived and she hurried to meet him. Her step faltered only very slightly when she saw that Doctor van der Tacx was with him. She had thought about him quite a lot since the night before, but somehow she hadn't expected to see him again. Mr Dale muttered something and glanced at them both, and the Dutch doctor said at once: 'We've met already,' and smiled at her, then transferred his attention to Mr Dale again. Toby joined them then and they all went off to take a look at Commander Frost. After they had examined him, Mr Dale said: 'All right, Staff Nurse, we shall just have a little chat—there's no need for you to wait.'

Her 'Very well, sir,' was brisk as she made herself scarce, but his words sounded an ominous note in her ears; little chats usually meant bad news delivered in a carefully wrapped up way so as not to alarm the patient, but she doubted very much if the Commander would stand for that. And she was right, for doing a dressing on the other side of the ward presently, she could hear the old gentleman voicing his opinion about something or other in no uncertain manner, followed by Mr Dale's surprisingly conciliatory voice and the deeper murmur of the Dutch doctor. Presently they came from behind the curtains and in answer to Mr Dale's demand for her presence, Philomena handed over to the nurse assisting her, and led the three men into the office.

'Operating this afternoon, Philly,' said Mr Dale, who

had called her Philly unofficially for years.
'Commander Frost—hasn't a chance unless I do, and
not much of a one then. Better than lingering on, though.
Bronchus quite useless on the right side and the left
rapidly worsening.' He looked round him and enquired:
'Coffee?'

She whisked out of the little room, put her head
round the kitchen door with an urgent message for a tray
of coffee, and went back, while Mr Dale continued,
just as though he had never interrupted himself: 'He'll
be last on the list—what have I got?'

She told him. It wasn't a long list, luckily; the
Commander would go to theatre at four o'clock.
'There's just one thing,' went on Mr Dale, 'he refuses
to go anywhere but here afterwards. You'll have to fix
that…off duty then?'

'No,' said Philomena in a carefully cheerful voice,
'I shall be here.'

'Good—he'd like you to be there with him. Stretch
a point for once and stay on for a while, will you?
There won't be much to do—usual recovery stuff. Got
enough nurses?'

'I daresay the night staff will be on by the time he's
recovered,' she pointed out sensibly.

The coffee arrived just then and she said quietly:
'Unless you want me for anything else, sir, would you
excuse me? Dinners…'

'Of course.' And as she reached the door which

Doctor van der Tacx was holding open for her, 'Philly, the Commander hasn't a chance, you know, but he wants me to operate.'

She said 'Yes, sir, I understand,' and slipped past Doctor van der Tacx with no more than the briefest of glances.

She took the old man to theatre herself, holding the thin bony hand in hers as she walked beside the trolley, and when, in the anaesthetic room, he said in the commanding voice the pre-med hadn't quite dimmed: 'You will be with me when I wake, Philly,' she said in her calm way: 'Yes, I'll be there, Commander.' He had never called her Philly before.

The anaesthetist came in then; Doctor van der Tacx. She supposed that she should have felt surprise, but he seemed to be popping up all over the place, and besides, she was worrying about the Commander.

He came back from the recovery room just after seven o'clock, looking like a bad reprint of himself, and the nurse who had accompanied him handed Philomena the chart with a small expressive shrug. As she helped Philomena with the tubes and drips and all the paraphernalia attached to him, she remarked: 'He's not round, Philly. Mr Dale said he was to be returned to you before he regained consciousness; the rest's as well as can be expected. Mr Dale's been in to see him; he's coming here presently. Who's the anaesthetist? A super heartthrob, even Sister smiled at him.'

Philomena was frowning over Mr Dale's frightful

writing on the chart. 'Oh, he's a friend or something...I say, is this a two or a three? Why didn't someone teach Mr Dale to write?'

The nurse went and Philomena hurried back to the Commander, sat down by the bed and began to fill in the last of the day report. The ward was quiet now, the other operation cases were sleeping, the patients who had been allowed up being got back into their beds, she could hear their cheerful talk among themselves and the quieter voices of the nurses. The men were a little subdued, though; the Commander had been in the ward for a long time and they all liked the peppery old man.

He hadn't roused when the night staff came on duty. Philomena left a nurse with him and whisked into the office to give the report, and that done: 'I'm going to stay with Commander Frost for a bit,' she explained to Mary Blake who was taking over from her. 'I promised I would.'

Mary was pinning the drug keys to her starched front. 'OK, Philly—shall I let Night Sister know?'

But there was no need of that. Miss Cook, the Night Superintendent, already knew, for the telephone rang at that moment and her unhurried voice informed Mary that she had been informed of the Commander's operation and that Staff Nurse Parsons was to remain as long as she thought fit.

'Well, I never!' declared Philly. 'Fancy him remembering to let her know...'

'He didn't—Doctor van someone or other did—he anaesthetised, didn't he? I met Jill as I was coming on duty and she said the whole theatre had fallen for him.'

Philomena sped back down the ward, whispered a goodnight to the nurse who had been relieving her and bent over her patient; he was about to wake up, her experienced eye told her, and a moment later he opened his eyes, focussed them on her and demanded in a thread of a voice why they didn't get on with it.

'They have,' she told him serenely. 'It's all done and over and you're in your own bed again. All you have to do is to lie quiet and do what we ask of you.'

He gave a weak snort. 'What's the time?'

'Evening. Are you in any pain, Commander Frost?'

He shook his head. 'Can't feel a thing—feel most peculiar, too.'

'One always does. Will you close your eyes and sleep for a little while?'

'You'll be here?'

'Yes—not all night, of course, but for a while yet.'

He nodded. 'Just like my Lucy,' he muttered, and closed his eyes.

Mr Dale came half an hour later and Doctor van der Tacx with him. They looked at Philomena's carefully maintained observation chart, took a pulse she hadn't been able to get for several minutes, asked a few complicated questions of her in quiet voices and bent over their patient. Presently they straightened up again and

Mr Dale said in a perfectly ordinary voice: 'You'll be here for a while, Philly? I'll speak to someone and see if I can get a nurse to take over presently until you come back on duty in the morning.'

They were all watching their patient, aware that although his eyes were shut, he could hear them quite well. 'That suits me very well, sir,' said Philomena matter-of-factly. 'Is there anything special for the morning?'

A question Mr Dale answered rather more elaborately than he needed to; they all knew that Commander Frost wasn't going to be there in the morning, and when he had finished and wished her goodnight he said goodnight to his patient too, adding that he would see him in the morning when he would probably be feeling a good deal better.

After the two men had gone, Philomena sat down again and took the Commander's hand in hers, and he opened his eyes and smiled at her and then winked. She winked back. 'You old fraud,' she said, 'you were listening. Listeners never hear any good of themselves.'

He gave a tiny cackle of laughter. 'Only when they're meant to. Don't let my hand go, Philly.'

And she didn't, she held it, feeling the warmth leaving it as he slipped deeper and deeper into unconsciousness, until she knew that it didn't matter any more whether she held it or not.

It was almost eleven o'clock when she finally left the ward; she had done what she had to do in a composed manner, bidden the night staff goodbye and left quietly. Only when she was in the dim silent passage and going down the staircase did the tears begin to fall. By the time she had reached the ground floor and the empty echoing entrance hall she was sobbing silently in real earnest, impatiently smearing the tears over her tired cheeks as she went. At least it was so late that there would be no one about.

She was wrong of course. She hadn't seen him standing quietly at the side of the bottom step of the staircase; she walked right into him and only then stopped to lift a woebegone face and say: 'Oh, so sorry,' and then: 'Oh, it's you…'

'Yes. When did you last eat?'

It seemed a strange question, coming out of the blue like that, but she answered obediently: 'I had a cup of tea…'

'I said eat, Philly.'

'Well…' She sucked in her breath like a child and thought. 'I couldn't go to dinner—I couldn't leave the ward, you see, no trained staff…and at supper time I—I was with the Commander.' Two large tears rolled down her cheeks and she added: 'So sorry,' and wiped them away with the back of her hand.

His 'Come along,' was firm and kindly and she made no protest as they went through the main door. His car was close by, he opened the door and stuffed her gently into the seat, then got in beside her and drove out into

the almost deserted streets. He didn't go far; the neigh-
bourhood was a shabby one, full of Victorian houses
converted into flats and bedsitters, with a pub on every
corner and a fish and chip shop every few hundred
yards. He pulled up outside one of these and turned to
look at her. 'You'll feel better when you've eaten something,' he said placidly, 'and you can have it here.'

She spoke in a tired little voice. 'You're very kind,
but I don't think I could manage...'

She felt his arm, large and comforting, gently
drawing her head down on to his shoulder. 'There, there,
my pretty,' he said in a comforting voice, and she
thought: He must be blind or hasn't looked at me; she
was only too well aware that when she cried she looked
a quite pitiful object, with a red nose, puffy eyelids and
an unhappy tendency to hiccough. Her giggle was
watery. 'I'm not, you know—I look an absolute fright
when I howl.'

He took her chin in one hand and turned her face deliberately to the light. 'A pretty face is a poor substitute
for compassion and loving kindness—you'll do very
well as you are.' He took his arm away and opened the
door. 'I'll only be a few minutes.'

He was back in less than that, two newspaper-
wrapped, fragrant-smelling parcels balanced in one
hand. In the car once more, he unwrapped one and set
it carefully on her lap. 'I'm not quite sure which fish it
is, but chips are chips anywhere in the world. Eat up,

there's a good girl.' He unwrapped his own supper, and the sight of him, sitting back comfortably eating it with his fingers as though he did it every day of his life, somehow made everything seem normal again. Philomena tried a chip and found it good. Before long she had polished off her impromptu supper and her white face wasn't white any more, even though it was still blotchy from her crying.

The doctor ate the last chip and licked a large finger. 'It was better this way, you know,' he remarked. 'The Commander would have lived for only a short time without operation and so deeply drugged that he wouldn't have known what was happening. When that was pointed out to him he swore some very naval oaths and insisted upon operation. I think he was right, too.' He took the empty paper from her lap and rolled it up neatly. 'He liked you, Philomena.'

She felt much better; it was a relief to talk too. 'Yes, I think he did. My father was a bit peppery too...'

She found herself talking, still sad about the Commander, but able to talk about him, and presently she was telling the doctor about her father too. She hadn't talked about him for a long time; her stepmother and sisters spoke of him seldom, not because they hadn't loved him in their own fashion, but because his death had spoiled the pleasant tenor of their lives. The doctor listened, interpolating a remark now and again as though he were interested, and gradually she began to feel better, almost cheerful again. It was the fish and chip shop shutting its doors which roused her to think of the time, and when she saw that it was midnight she gave a gasp of horror. 'The time! Why didn't you say something—you must be longing for your bed instead of sitting here listening to me boring on about someone you never met...'

'I've not been bored and I'm certainly not tired, indeed I've enjoyed your company.'

'You couldn't have,' burst out Philomena. 'Just look at me!'

Which he did, taking his time about it. 'I'm looking,' he said at length, 'and I like what I see.'

She could think of nothing to say to that as he started the car and drove back to the hospital, saying nothing much himself. He wished her a quiet good-night at its entrance and made no reference to meeting her again. As she got ready for bed she thought it very unlikely that she would see him—he had been more than kind for the second time within a week, but cir-cumstances had made their meetings inevitable, although it struck her now that he might have been waiting for her as she had gone off duty that evening. She dismissed the idea, though; after all, he was pre-sumably working in the hospital for a short time—probably with Mr Dale. They seemed to know each other very well, and what was more likely than that they should meet occasionally?

Contrary to her expectations, she slept immediately her head touched the pillow.

She saw nothing of him the next day, although one of her friends, the theatre staff nurse, assured her that he was anaesthetising for Mr Dale again, and on the next day he had gone.

A week later she went home—it was Chloe's birthday; she was to have a party, a big one to celebrate the fact that she was eighteen. Philomena had a long weekend for it and had bought a new dress; cream silk with a high neck and long sleeves and a full skirt. It was trimmed with narrow lace and was, she considered, exactly right for the occasion; Chloe and Miriam would look enchanting in whatever they wore; they always did, and she knew that it would be quite impossible to rival them; she wouldn't have dreamed of doing so, anyway. She put on her nicely cut grey flannel suit, tossed her raincoat over her arm, picked up her overnight bag, and took a taxi to the station.

There was no one to meet her at Wareham station, although she had telephoned the day before to say that she was coming, so she took a taxi to the charming Georgian house by the river. There was no one home, only Molly, the housekeeper, who had been with them for such a long time that Philomena couldn't remember life without her. She came from the kitchen as she went in, wiping her hands on a towel, her nice wrinkled face beaming with pleasure.

'Miss Philly, how lovely to see you—the Missus and Miss Chloe and Miss Miriam have gone over to Bournemouth to get something or other—they said you wouldn't mind getting yourself here. They'll be back by teatime.' She glanced at Philomena's disappointed face. 'So you've passed those exams of yours, you clever girl. How proud your dad would have been of you—just as I am, Miss Philly.' She took the bag from Philomena's hand. 'I've a nice little lunch all ready for you—you just come into the kitchen and eat it, there's a good girl.'

It was a very nice lunch and Molly was interested in her hospital life; she stood at the other end of the big kitchen table, making pastry and plying Philomena with questions, so that very shortly Philomena began to feel a good deal more cheerful, and presently, when she had unpacked in her pretty bedroom overlooking the river, she went downstairs and strolled through the garden to the water's edge until Molly called her in for tea, and soon after that her stepmother and sisters came home. They embraced her warmly, all talking at once about the party, and swept her upstairs to admire their dresses, and it wasn't until they were going to their rooms to tidy themselves for dinner that her stepmother observed carelessly: 'Did you pass your exams, Philly? I do hope so—so boring for you, darling, I can't think why you want to stay at that horrid hospital. Which reminds me, Nicholas Pierce and his wife have asked us all to lunch tomorrow—so convenient, because we shall have enough to do with the party without feeding ourselves. We're to meet them at the Priory Hotel at half past twelve. I hope you've got something smart to wear?'

'My suit—there's that silk blouse I left at home—I could wear that with it…no hat.'

Her stepmother glanced at Philomena's neat head of hair. 'No? Well, dear, I don't suppose it makes much difference. The suit's all right.' She smiled, already thinking about something else. 'See you downstairs, Philly.'

The evening passed quickly. There were last-minute plans to make, local gossip to mull over, the question as to whether Chloe should have her curly dark hair dressed in a different style discussed at length. They were on their way to bed when her stepmother remembered to ask Philomena again: 'Did you pass, darling? Not that it matters I expect.'

Philomena paused on the stairs. 'Yes, Mother, I passed.' She didn't add that it had mattered very much.

'I suppose everyone celebrated?' asked Chloe.

'Yes,' said Philomena, 'it's customary.'

'How nice,' remarked Mrs Parsons a little vaguely. 'I expect you have lots of friends. No one special, I suppose?'

Philomena had a sudden vivid memory of a large, fair man with kind blue eyes. She said, 'No,' feeling regret as she said it.

She was up early; it had tacitly been agreed for some time now that as she rose early at the hospital, she should do the same at home, and while her stepmother and sisters had trays taken to their rooms by a hard-working Molly, she had formed the habit of eating her own breakfast with the housekeeper in the kitchen. And Molly, who found this unfair, made it up to her by dishing up a splendid meal of eggs and bacon, marmalade and toast and all the coffee she cared to drink, besides which she saw to it that Philomena had a news-paper to read while she ate. Usually she didn't have much to say, but this morning, with the party looming, they talked. Miriam had a new boy-friend, a young man whom Molly described severely as nothing but a playboy: 'Loaded with money,' she added with a snort, 'and spends it all on himself.' She sniffed with disap-proval. 'Them as 'as money should know how to use it.' She slapped the toast rack down with something of a thump. 'Miss Miriam's fair set on 'im—and so's yer ma.' She poured more coffee for Philomena. 'And Miss Chloe, eighteen today, and just thrown over another young man—she's begun too early if you ask me.'

Philomena buttered more toast and spread it with Molly's homemade marmalade. 'Well, you know, girls seem to grow up more quickly nowadays,' she observed with all the wisdom of twenty-three years, 'and perhaps this boy-friend of Miriam's really loves her—after all, if he's all that rich he's got to lavish his money on someone other than himself.'

The housekeeper regarded her with loving scorn.

'The trouble is with you, Miss Philly, you're too nice—just like yer own ma—she weren't no beauty, just like you, but nice enough to eat.'

And Philomena, recognising this as a great compliment from one who seldom uttered them, thanked her, adding a hug and a kiss on an elderly cheek by way of extras.

She spent the morning arranging the flowers, because she was good at it and as her stepmother pointed out, it was such a waste of money to employ someone to do it when Philly was so conveniently home, and then there were last-minute errands to run, the telephone to answer, and the buffet supper, a labour of love on Molly's part, to check. The drinks Mrs Parsons had left to Mr Pierce; he would bring them round after they had all lunched at the Priory. 'And for heaven's sake hurry up and get dressed,' begged Mrs Parsons, quite unmindful that until that moment Philly hadn't had a moment to herself. 'I want you to go on ahead, darling, and pop into Mr Timms' and make sure he sends the icecream.' She added: 'We'll meet you at the hotel.'

So Philomena dressed, far too quickly so that her face had less attention than usual and her hair was screwed back in a rather careless knot, and hurried round to Mr Timms', who was inclined to be hurt at the very idea of Mrs Parsons thinking that he might forget such an important order. Philomena said all she should have and, with time to spare, went straight to the hotel.

The Pierces weren't there yet, of course; Mr Gee, the owner, met her in the entrance and when they had passed the time of day, suggested that she might like to stroll through the gardens and take a look at the river. So she did that, wandering round the side of the lovely old building, with its small arched doorways and court-yards and coming eventually to the gardens. It was a bright day with a blue sky from which the sun shone without much warmth, and the gardens looked beauti-ful; tulips and late daffodils and hyacinths jostled for a place among the shrubs. Philomena took the narrow path which bordered the grounds and came to the river. There were no boats out, it was too early in the year still, but the swans were gliding along the further bank and the water looked clear and very clean. She was contem-plating the scene when Doctor van der Tacx said 'Hullo,' from somewhere behind her and she spun round, green eyes wide in a plain face rendered more plain than it need have been by reason of the chilly little wind coming off the water. 'It's you!' she ex-claimed idiotically, and failed to see the amused gleam in his eyes.

'In person.' He went on smoothly: 'Some friends told me what a very pleasant place this was for a few days' peace and quiet; I arrived only a few minutes ago and happened to see you crossing the garden.' His smile was charming and she found herself smiling back at him. 'Of course, you live here…'

She nodded. 'Yes—just down the river a little way—we're here for lunch with friends of my stepmother's.' She glanced at her watch and felt reluctance to go. 'They'll be here—I came on early, I had a message to deliver.'

He turned away from the river. 'We'll walk back together. Have you a long holiday?'

'A long weekend. Have you been here before?'

He shook his head. 'I seldom get further afield than London, I'm afraid, but it just so happens that I had a few days to spare.' He glanced at her. 'Is this a celebration lunch?'

It was silly to feel hurt still; she said cheerfully: 'Oh, no—it's my youngest stepsister's birthday.' She had expected him to wish her goodbye when they reached the hotel again; they had walked round to the newer side of the old place, Regency and charming with its wide windows and doors and borders of spring flowers. They went in through the open drawing room door together and found her stepmother and sisters and Mr and Mrs Pierce standing there, watching them from the French window, and Philomena, who had been enjoying herself more than she could have supposed in the doctor's company, took a sideways look at his face and felt her pleasure ebb; he had caught sight of Chloe and Miriam and was reacting just as all the other men, old and young, did. And she couldn't blame him; they looked quite lovely; their vivid, dark beauty set off exactly by the clothes they were wearing, their lovely faces delicately made up. She felt a thrill of pride at the sight of them, mixed with regret that she couldn't, just for a day, be as breathtakingly lovely.

It was her stepmother who spoke first. 'Darling, we wondered where you were—we were getting quite anxious.' An absurd remark considering she had herself told Philomena to meet them there at the hotel, but nicely calculated, thought Philomena, to give a motherly and loving impression. And I'm growing to be pretty mean, she told herself, and smiled with extra warmth to make up for it.

'Sorry, dears—I went down to have a look at the river. I met Doctor van der Tacx there—he's been at Faith's. Mother...' She made the introductions with an unconscious charm and felt wry amusement at Chloe's and Miriam's instant reactions. They were used to men finding them attractive and normally they didn't pay much attention to them, accepting their admiration as their due, but in the doctor they saw someone rather different. Any girl would be more than delighted to have him dancing attendance. Philomena, exchanging small talk with Mr and Mrs Pierce, heard Miriam inviting him to the party and Chloe chiming in asking him to join them at lunch.

She supposed it was mean of her to be pleased when he declined lunch, even a drink, pleading a previous engagement, but her pleasure was short-lived because her stepmother added her own persuasive voice to Miriam's and before he left them he had promised to come to the party that evening. His goodbyes were made a few minutes later. His manners were nice, thought Philomena, although he might have offered her rather more than the casual nod he gave her. Although, come to think of it, why should he when Chloe and Miriam were there to distract him from anyone and anything else?

During lunch she was questioned a good deal about him in a good-natured fashion. 'Did he know that you were here?' asked Chloe.

Philomena shook her head. 'No, it was pure chance—someone told him the Priory was a splendid place to stay at and so he came here.'

'And of course,' remarked her stepmother with unintentional cruelty, 'you wouldn't have known him very well at Faith's, would you? You're hardly his kind of girl.'

A home truth which needed to be swallowed with as good a grace as she could manage. It was Mrs Pierce who changed the conversation to the all-important one of the party, and Mr Pierce who asked the attentive manager to bring another bottle of claret, both of which actions helped Philomena considerably in the regaining of her usual calm.

CHAPTER THREE

PHILOMENA HAD LITTLE TIME to think about the doctor during the afternoon. There were a dozen and one jobs to do, and as Chloe and Miriam, after helping her for an hour or so, cried off, declaring that they would be fit for nothing unless they put their feet up for the rest of the afternoon, she was kept busy until well after teatime. It was her stepmother, coming down from her room to make sure that the preparations were complete, who found her arranging the buffet supper in the dining room and told her to leave what she was doing and get herself dressed.

'Well, I will if there's someone free to finish this,' agreed Philomena. But there wasn't—Molly, reinforced by the daily woman, was busy in the kitchen, and both girls were still in their rooms, and as her stepmother pointed out with lazy good nature, she herself was quite incapable of arranging things on plates.

'You'll just have to hurry up, darling,' she observed

pleasantly. 'Luckily you never take long to dress, do you?' She paused as she was about to go out of the room, frowning a little. 'I hope you've got something pretty to wear. Chloe has that apricot crêpe and Miriam is wearing leaf green—you saw them—for heaven's sake don't clash with them.'

'I won't,' Philomena assured her. 'I played safe—it's cream silk and quite unobtrusive.'

'Oh, good. How thoughtful of you, darling—you're such a nice girl, Philly—such a pity you haven't your sisters' looks.'

And half an hour later Philomena heartily agreed with her, looking at her reflection in the long wall mirror in her pretty bedroom. The dress was pretty but not in the least eye-catching, although did she but know it, its demure simplicity was flattering to her pretty figure and its creamy whiteness served as a splendid contrast to her green eyes. But she didn't see this, only that her long fine hair hadn't a curl in it and her nose and mouth were quite nondescript. But there wasn't much time to waste on her appearance; Chloe had given her a bottle of *Vu* perfume which she hadn't cared for herself, and Philomena sprayed it on her person with a discreet hand, happily unaware that it didn't suit her at all, and sped downstairs just in time to greet the first guests, lead them to the big sitting room and offer them drinks. Her stepmother and the girls were in the hall, the three of them making a quite startlingly lovely picture grouped together in an eye-catching pose as the guests entered the house. Philomena knew exactly the effect they would have on Doctor van der Tacx when he arrived, and she was proved correct; for he made his way across the crowded room when he caught sight of her and after a casual 'Hullo,' remarked: 'What remarkably pretty girls your sisters are—they quite take one's breath.'

Philomena eyed him calmly, reflecting that as far as she was concerned she might as well have been wearing a sack. 'They're quite beautiful,' she agreed serenely. 'And they're clever and kind, too,' she added for good measure and not quite truthfully. 'They're not a bit conceited, either.'

He stood looking down at her, very handsome in his dinner jacket, half smiling. 'But they haven't green eyes,' he observed quietly as he studied her in a leisurely fashion. 'I like your dress—it's pretty and suits you…' He saw her eyes flash and added: 'I did that badly, didn't I? Forgive me; to admire your sisters and ignore you—I suppose I felt that I didn't need to tell you…'

'You don't need to tell me anything.' She strove to keep her voice cool and faintly amused. 'You forget that I've been their sister for a long time; if you didn't admire them I should feel quite annoyed with you.'

He raised his eyebrows. 'What an unnatural girl you are not to wish for admiration for yourself.'

She longed to tell him just how much she did wish it, but what would be the use? To stir up pity and rekindle the kindness he had shown her? She said tartly: 'You must think I'm a halfwit to wish any such thing.' Then she smiled brightly at him. 'Come and meet some of our friends—we're going to dance in the drawing room presently.'

She led him round the room and presently Miriam joined them, saying that she would take him under her wing. 'As I expect you and Philly see enough of each other in hospital; working with people isn't at all the same as knowing them socially, is it?' she asked gaily. 'If we leave you together I suppose you'll only talk about operations and people being ill, I'm sure that's all you have in common.'

Philomena said nothing but smiled a little and slid away to talk to old Mrs Glenville, who was really too elderly for parties but was too much a family friend to leave out, and when they all trooped into the drawing room presently she immediately accepted Mr Pierce's invitation to partner him, trying not to notice that Miriam and Doctor van der Tacx were dancing together and looking quite the handsomest couple in the room, and later when she saw him take Chloe out on to the verandah which ran the length of the long room, she pretended not to see that too.

But it was Miriam he danced with most; the evening was more than half over before he made his way across the floor and asked Philomena to dance. She would have liked to refuse him, but she had no excuse, and besides, she warned herself, it would have been childish to have done so—and what, in heaven's name, did she expect? So she accepted gaily and gyrated and shrugged her way through the next ten minutes; she didn't much like dancing by herself; she supposed she was old-fashioned, but to her way of thinking, waltzing or foxtrotting with an agreeable partner was preferable to turning and twisting opposite each other with little or no chance to talk. Apparently the doctor felt the same way, for suddenly he stretched out a long arm and plucked her away from the twirling dancers and walked her out to the verandah. Once there he sat her down on one of the cane benches, said: 'That's better,' and settled himself beside her.

'Splendid exercise,' he observed mildly, 'but I'm too large for it. I prefer something more restful—sailing or skating.'

'Have you a boat?' she asked.

'Oh, yes—I potter around the Friesian lakes whenever I have the leisure in the summer. Do you sail, Philomena?'

'Only a dinghy.'

'And skate?'

'Ice skating, you mean?' She shook her head. 'I'd love to, though, it looks so easy.'

'It is. When do you go back to Faith's?'

'The day after tomorrow.'

'I'll drive you up—I have to be there myself.'

Philomena hesitated; there was nothing she would like better, but he had said that he was on holiday. Perhaps he didn't have to return quite so soon, perhaps he was just being kind again...

'That's settled, then,' he said comfortably without waiting for her to answer, and then: 'You should be sharing the glory with Chloe, shouldn't you?'

'Me? It's not my birthday... Oh, you mean because I passed my Finals.'

'Yes, I did mean that. I hear that you are also Gold Medallist for the year—are you keeping that a secret too?'

She said sharply: 'I'm not keeping it a secret—it's not important compared with Chloe's birthday.'

He turned to look at her in the dim light. 'Didn't anyone ask you?' he asked her quietly.

How tiresome he was with his questions! 'Well, they had a lot to think about,' she mumbled lamely.

'Indeed, yes.'

The dancing had stopped for the moment and it was very quiet until Doctor van der Tacx told her with shattering frankness: 'You're wearing the wrong kind of perfume—much too sophisticated for you, Philomena. Did you choose it?'

She was too taken aback to be annoyed. 'Well, no— Chloe had it given to her and she didn't like it. It's French and very expensive.'

'And on the right person, quite delightful.'

'But not me,' she said in a small voice.

'Not you, Philly. I...' He paused as the door was flung wide and Miriam and a young man came out. 'Here they are!' she cried. 'I guessed you'd be here, discussing the latest thing in broken bones, I suppose.' She gave her companion a push. 'Take Philly in to supper, Bill. I'll see that Walle gets his, but first I want to show him the river from the bottom of the garden.'

That was the last Philomena saw of him, except for a rather vague goodnight when he said goodbye to Mrs Parsons. Chloe and Miriam were there too, of course, as the guests went home, and he wasn't vague with either of them, she was quick to notice. Indeed, Miriam was clinging to his arm and whispering to him—it must have been something very amusing, because he laughed down at her in what Philomena considered to be a quite besotted fashion.

She was up early in the morning, helping Molly to get the house straight again, taking trays up to her stepmother and sisters, helping Molly to prepare the lunch, but presently when she had done these things she got into slacks and a sweater, told Molly that she was going riding, and left the house. There was a riding stables close by and Mr Stiles who owned it was a good friend of hers; Bessy, the little grey mare she always rode, was saddled for her and she went out of the town towards Holton Heath. There was little traffic, it was still too early in the year for that, and what weekend traffic there was on its way to Bournemouth had passed through the

day before. Only one car passed her as she crossed the
Wool road from the stables to take a bridle path circum-
venting the town—a Khamsin with the doctor at the
wheel. He was going in the direction of her home and
she thought wryly that he would be lucky if he didn't
have to wait at least an hour for Miriam, since it would
be she he was going to see. He braked hard when he saw
her, but she didn't stop, only raised a gloved hand in
casual salute before she turned Bessy's nose into the
bridle path.

She didn't get back home until almost teatime, to
find her stepmother and sisters out and Molly in the
kitchen with her feet up taking a well-earned rest. 'Your
ma's gone to the Pierces', Miss Chloe went out after
lunch with a bunch of young people, and Miss Miriam
went out with that doctor.' She peeped at Philomena as
she spoke. 'He didn't sound too keen to take her, but
she's always able to get her own way. They said cold
supper as they didn't know when they would be back.
There's a nice tea for you, Miss Philly, you go along and
change and I'll bring it along to the sitting room. Are
you going to be in for supper?'

Philomena nodded. 'I think so, Molly—I'll go to
church and then come straight back here. I must pack
too…'

It struck her suddenly that she had no idea at what
time Doctor van der Tacx intended leaving. She was on
duty at two o'clock the next day, she would have to

leave fairly early in the morning, if he didn't know that, and come to think of it, she hadn't told him, he might have arranged to leave himself much later in the day, in which case she would have to go by train. She went upstairs and bathed and changed into her suit, and presently ate a splendid tea round the fire in the sitting room before going to rummage through her cupboards to find a hat for church.

She sat in the family pew towards the front of the lovely old church, and the service was just about to begin when Doctor van der Tacx slid into the seat beside her. Beyond smiling at her he said nothing; she had no idea if he was as surprised as she was, and there was no way of finding out. He joined in the service in the most natural manner possible and when it was over walked with her to the door and stood a moment in the porch. It was a quiet spring evening, though a little chilly, and the Priory Hotel, a stone's throw away, had welcoming lights at its entrance. 'Will eight o'clock suit you?' asked the doctor suddenly. 'You're on duty at two o'clock, aren't you? I went to see you this morning but you—er—didn't stop.'

Philomena was surprised at the surge of pleasure his words engendered. She said slowly: 'I didn't know you wanted to speak to me—I thought...' she paused; if she said that he would think she was envious of her sisters, and she wasn't. 'Eight o'clock would do fine—do you want me to meet you here?'

'I'll come for you.' He looked as though he was going to say something else, but when he didn't she added a quiet 'Goodnight,' and smiled at him before crossing the little square in front of the church on her way home.

She was ready and waiting when the Khamsin crept to a halt before the door. She had said goodbye to her stepmother and sisters and they had opened sleepy eyes and smiled at her and murmured, 'Come home again soon, Philly,' and gone to sleep again before she was out of their rooms, and Molly, urging her to eat her breakfast, had been almost tearful. She was in the hall now, fussing a little, reminding her to do this, that and the other thing, to write, not to forget her old Molly. Philomena gave her an affectionate hug and thanked her for her lovely weekend because her stepmother hadn't heard when she had said that in her bedroom and she felt that someone should be thanked. She was glad to see how kind the doctor was to Molly; waiting patiently while the housekeeper delayed them with last-minute questions and then bidding her goodbye. 'Philly must love coming home to you,' he observed as he took her hand, and she watched her faithful old friend's face wreath itself in smiles.

They took the Wimborne Minster road, cutting across country along roads which Philomena was surprised to discover he knew. It was a clear morning, the early sunshine taking the chill off the night, and there wasn't much traffic. She made a few tentative remarks which her companion answered pleasantly enough, but without much encouragement, so that presently she lapsed into silence, a silence which he broke once they were on the A31, speeding towards the motorway.

'You sped away rather sharply after church,' he observed. 'I was about to ask you to have dinner with me at the hotel, but I didn't dare…'

'Didn't dare?' she repeated, astonished.

'You can be—what is the word?—daunting. I think I was afraid of being snubbed.'

She turned to look at him. 'But that's absurd! Why should I snub you?'

'I don't know—you tell me.'

'Well, I didn't mean to.' She added in a sudden burst of honesty: 'I thought you might think that I was waiting for you to give me a drink or walk home with me.'

'And you didn't want me to do either?' He shot past a cattle truck, slowed to bypass Ringwood and got up speed again as he took the road to Cadnam.

'Yes, I did. Isn't it a lovely morning? Did they mind giving you such an early breakfast at the Priory?'

'No, not in the least.' They were almost at the motorway now and he kept up a good speed, and as they joined it put his foot down, so that the powerful car shot forward along the almost empty road. He didn't say much until they were clear of the Winchester bypass and heading for Alresford.

'Are we going the right way?' asked Philomena.

'I thought coffee at the Bell in Alresford, we can go on from there to Alton and then run up to the M3.'

There was plenty of time; she agreed happily. It was while they were sitting in the coffee room of the old coaching inn that he asked: 'What are you going to do next?'

She spooned sugar into her cup. 'Oh, well—if I wait for a time, I can apply for a Sister's post. I expect I'll stay on Men's Surgical until then.'

'And when is then?'

'A year, perhaps—when there's a vacancy; someone getting married or retiring or going to another post— one never knows.'

He stared at her very hard. 'Would you consider another job? As a surgery nurse? I told you that I have two partners; the practice is big and covers a large country area. We each have our own consulting rooms as well as a clinic in Ommen and we all have beds in hospitals in Zwolle and Hoogeveen. I travel a good deal too. Our nurse is getting married and we need a replacement—we have a receptionist and a secretary and part-time help, but we can't manage without a nurse. Would you like to take the job for a time and see how you like it? You would be in Ommen because one of my partners has the clinic close to his house and that is mostly where you would work. He's married with children and a rather nice wife. The other partner lives at Dalfsen, and I live between the two near a village called Vilsteren. You could take over the rooms Ellie had and the salary would be much the same as you're getting at present.'

'The language...' Philomena pointed out breathlessly.

'We all speak English, so, to a certain extent, does the receptionist. Basic Dutch will be more than sufficient. Presumably you will have to give a month's notice at Faith's, so during that time you can take a few lessons.'

'You've thought of everything,' she said wonderingly.

'Er—I have given it some thought...'

'Why me?'

His reply was prompt and matter-of-fact. 'Mr Dale tells me that you are a first class nurse, but he also mentioned that there is no hope of a Sister's post for months to come. You might just as well have a change of occupation while you're waiting for it. You'll suit Theo de Klein, my partner, very well, he likes a sensible girl with no nonsense about her, and no immediate prospect of getting married—all the girls he has interviewed so far have boy-friends or want their evenings free.'

Philomena swallowed this frank statement as best she might while a strong and sudden desire to show the tiresome man that she was none of these things possessed her. Her serene expression didn't change, but her green eyes gleamed at an idea she had just that moment had.

She would take the job, presumably she would see something of the doctor from time to time and that would give her an opportunity to make him eat his words. It would be difficult, of course, because she was actually all the things he had described, but at least she would try...

She said in her sensible way: 'May I think it over? I rather like the idea, that is, of course, if your partners approve.'

'They will.' He sounded very positive. 'A trial period, perhaps, and if you like the work and everything else is satisfactory, we can come to some arrangement.'

She said slowly: 'Yes, I think so. You mentioned that the girls already interviewed wanted their evenings free...does that mean that there are clinics every evening?'

He looked a little surprised. 'Good lord, no—though evening surgery does go on till eight-ish. I think we agreed among ourselves that too much outside interest—coming in late, being late at work in the morning as a consequence—it just wouldn't do.'

'You want a girl with no other interest but her work and possibly a little reading and knitting in her free time.' She sounded tart, and he said at once:

'I put it badly—not made myself clear.'

'On the contrary, you made yourself very clear.' Philomena gave him a pleasant smile. 'Ought we to be going?'

He lifted a finger for the bill, looking at her. 'You will consider my offer? I go to Edinburgh tomorrow and I expect to be away about a week. Would that be long enough?'

She nodded. 'Telephone me when you get back.'

'I'll do better than that; if I may, I'll take you out for a meal.'

She rose from her chair and went composedly to the door. 'That would be nice. Thank you for the coffee.'

And after that the conversation was exclusively of the party, the charm of the hotel and Wareham and the extraordinary good looks of her stepsisters. 'They're quite gorgeous, aren't they?' she agreed cheerfully. 'I'm surprised every time I go home and I've known them for ten years, how they must strike someone who hasn't met them before is quite something.'

Doctor van der Tacx threw her a sidelong glance. 'It is. Is there a list this afternoon?'

They talked about the hospital and new techniques and the variety of patients they had encountered until they reached the outskirts of London, when he left the main road, weaving the car through the side streets until she exclaimed in some surprise: 'We're in the Brompton Road!'

'With time enough for lunch.'

He took her to the Brompton Grill and Philomena did full justice to the delicious meal: sole, with scampi sauce, tiny new potatoes and even tinier peas, and a whipped-up froth of cream and fruit for dessert, and because she would have to work that afternoon, a light dry wine which the doctor assured her would do her no harm at all.

They hadn't a great deal of time and the doctor didn't mention his suggestion that she should work for his partner again. Philomena occupied the short journey to the hospital with small talk delivered in a bright manner which she hoped concealed the splendid muddle of feelings jostling each other inside her. As they approached the narrow street which would take them round the back way to Faith's, she fell silent, compiling a graceful speech of thanks for her ride and her lunch, a speech which, however, she had no opportunity to make, for driving in through a side gate they were at once caught up in a tangle of ambulances, police cars and people.

'What on earth...' began Philomena, and then: 'There was that march this morning...'

The doctor slid the car between two ambulances with an inch to spare on either side, shot across the forecourt and parked with instant smoothness beside the Rolls-Royces, Daimlers and Jaguars belonging to the consultants. 'We'll soon see,' he observed with calm, and opened her door. They had just gained the front entrance when another ambulance, its light flashing, its siren wailing urgently, raced in. Potter, the Head Porter, was for once out of his little office, a paper in his hand, giving instructions to his team, but when he caught sight of them he broke off to say: 'Mr Dale was asking for you, sir—if you would go to the Accident Room and join him there, and Staff, Sister Brice left a message.

You're to go to the Accident Room and stay there until you're no longer required, and then you're to return to Men's Surgical.'

She nodded. 'OK, Potter, but what's happened?'

'That march—got out of hand, it seems—any number of casualties, and we're the nearest hospital.'

'Oh, lord—is the march still going on?'

He gave her a withering look; he was elderly and tired, and people had been asking questions all the morning. 'No, it's not, but the fighting is.'

Philomena was halfway to the nurses' home when she remembered that she hadn't said goodbye to Doctor van der Tacx, let alone thanked him for her lunch.

The Accident Room, when she reached it ten minutes later, was crowded and to a casual onlooker, chaos appeared to reign although this was not the case; the serious, the not so serious and the lightly wounded had been sifted, so that the bays at the end of the vast apartment were filled with stretchers whose unfortunate occupants were being examined by the various consultants and their registrars, dealt with and despatched to the wards or theatre, the larger bays which ran the length of the place were crammed with cut heads and faces, simple arm fractures, contusions and the like, and the remaining benches lining the walls taken up with minor injuries. Of course, to these were constantly added fresh patients, so that the coming and going was considerable, with Sister Curtis, who had spent her nursing life first in Casualty and then in the Accident Room, marshalling her forces with an expert hand. She buttonholed Philomena at once with instructions to station herself at the main doors and classify the cases as they came in. 'You're a sensible girl, so I'm told,' she observed in her forthright manner. 'Use your discretion and don't hesitate to get help if it's needed stat.'

So Philomena wormed her way through the mass of patients, most of them policemen, waiting their uncomplaining turns, and arrived at the doors just as another ambulance drew up.

It held four casualties; two policemen stretched out unconscious on their stretchers, both with ugly head wounds, and the two sitting patients, one an old lady with a cut hand, roughly bandaged, and the other a small boy with his arm in a sling. Neither of them said a word, just looked at her as they were shepherded into the Accident Room, and she sat them down with a murmur of assurance and turned back to the stretcher cases. One was a good deal worse than the other; black eye, broken nose, cut lip and a nasty jagged wound across the back of his head. Broken bottles, Philomena guessed, and probably a boot in the face; she had seen it before, and probably, she thought wearily, she would see it again. The second man was young, his fair hair full of fragments of glass, one cheek slashed and oozing sluggishly. She called a nurse over to help her and together they unbuttoned jackets, took off boots and began their careful search for bodily injuries, before sending them over to the swelling numbers of seriously injured. 'And stay a bit,' cautioned Philomena to the nurse, 'make sure that someone knows that they're there; they do need warding quickly.' She smiled at the two porters as she turned back to her other two patients.

It was difficult to know which one to attend to first. The small boy was crying now, but the old lady, although she wasn't complaining, had become alarmingly pale. Philomena started to talk to the child while she eased off the old lady's coat. Probably there was some other injury as well as the cut on her hand, which was nasty enough but hardly warranted the pallor. She cleaned and dressed the wound with gentle efficiency, laid the old lady down on the stretcher the porters had brought back, took a decidedly poor pulse and asked cheerfully: 'Did you have a nasty shock, my dear? Were you pushed or bumped or knocked down?' and while she talked she probed gently for broken bones.

'Got pushed around,' muttered her patient, 'knocked about somethink shockin'—me ribs 'urt, Nurse.'

A clue to be followed up. Philomena took a close look under the cardigan; there was a small slit in the brightly patterned blouse, easily overlooked, just as the faint bloodstains round it were almost invisible. And underneath the blouse there was another slit. Philomena delved gently and presently found what she had expected; a small almost hidden stab wound just under the old lady's ribs, its lips curled in nastily; such a small cut, but probably it had done a good deal of damage. Philomena slid a sterile pad over it, talking soothingly while she did so, and signed to the porters. 'This one's urgent,' she whispered as she scribbled a note. 'Give that to someone at once—Mr Dale if you can get at him, if not, his registrar.' She smiled at the old lady. 'That's a nasty bump on your ribs,' she warned her. 'If they want you to stay here for the night and rest, is there anyone you want us to tell?'

The old lady shook her head. 'Ain't got no one,' she muttered. 'I'd dearly like a good sleep.'

'Not to worry, we'll look after you.' Philomena squeezed the rather grubby hand and sent the porters on their way, then went back to the small boy. The ward clerk was there, coaxing his name and address from him. 'He can't remember the name of the road,' she said worriedly. 'Tall chimneys at the end of it, he says, and a pub in the middle.'

'Pickett's Lane,' said Philomena promptly as she slid the sling off the small bony arm, 'about five minutes' walk from here. What's your dad's name, love?'

'Merrow.' The child suddenly burst into tears. '"E won't 'arf tear inter me, 'e told me not ter go inter the street.'

Philomena was putting the sling back on again; a simple Colles' fracture which could be put into plaster without further ado. 'He'll be so glad to see you back I don't suppose he'll be at all cross,' she soothed him.

'You go with this nice porter and they'll have you as right as rain in no time,' and as he was led away: 'See if you can get hold of a bobby to send someone round to Pickett's Lane and fetch his dad here, will you, Jean?' and as the clerk sped away, Philomena straightened out the trolley and turned to receive the next load from the arriving ambulance.

And so the day wore on; it was long past teatime before the last of the casualties had been dealt with. The Accident Room emptied itself slowly and a fresh batch of nurses moved in to take over. Philomena, a little untidy by now, straightened her cap and repaired to Men's Surgical; she was on duty until eight o'clock and there was still an hour or more to go. She plodded up the stairs, wondering what was for supper, reflecting that lunch seemed a long time ago. She had seen Walle van der Tacx once or twice in the Accident Room, looming head and shoulders above everyone else, but always at a distance, and when she had had the chance to look around her, there had been no sign of him. She sighed and opened the doors of Men's Surgical.

Sister Brice was on duty and in a towering rage; the ward was choc-a-bloc for a start, a number of nurses from other less busy wards had been sent to help her and as they weren't 'her' nurses, she naturally disapproved of them, and the inevitable untidiness of the ward caused by the sudden influx of new patients had irritated her to a state of snappishness, making life difficult enough for the nurses without the burden of the extra work with which they were coping. Philomena, called into the office to be given a spate of orders, received the full brunt of her superior's wrath. She received it meekly, as there was no point in getting the poor woman more upset than she already was, and when Sister Brice paused at last for breath, suggested that a nice cup of coffee might ease her feelings. 'Dora's in the kitchen still,' said Philomena helpfully, 'and I know she'll make you one at once. I'll ask her on the way in.'

Dora, smarting from Sister's tongue, wasn't disposed to be co-operative. 'Why her?' she demanded. 'You all deserve a cup. I don't see…'

'Dear Dora,' wheedled Philomena, 'how thoughtful you are—of course we'd all like a cup, but we're off in another hour and Sister will have to write the report and give it. She'll be ages after us—be a darling.'

Dora made a face. 'OK, since it's for you, Staff, but I'm not saying I'm doing it willingly.'

'That's what makes you a darling,' said Philomena.

It was almost nine o'clock before she got off duty. Sister needed help—she couldn't write the report and give it and be sure that the ward was adequately covered at the same time; Philomena must stay until the night staff were free to take over. So she stayed, to go down to the dining room presently to a supper which an hour earlier had been nice enough but which was by now dried on its plate. She begged bread and butter from the canteen maid and carried it off with her to her room, where various of her friends waited with tea and an assortment of food; potato crisps, someone's birthday cake, some rather stale biscuits, and a bag of toffees, stuck together. Philomena ate her starved way through anything offered to her and then sat down on the bed to compose a note to the doctor; she still had to thank him for her lunch and the lift back. They seemed a long time ago now. She took it down to the porter's lodge presently, with instructions to Potter to give it to Doctor van der Tacx if he should see him. Potter's rather stern features confronted her through his little window. 'Well, I will do that, Staff, though I don't know what's coming to all you young persons nowadays—nurses writing notes to senior members of the medical profession!'

She pushed her cap straight on her untidy head. 'Potter dear, it's a bread and butter letter—you know...he gave me a lift up from my home and we had lunch, so of course I have to thank him—we didn't have time when we got here, now did we?'

He relaxed a little. 'Well, that's different, Staff. I'll let him have it. He's still in the hospital, up in theatre.'

The news made her feel happier, although she didn't know why. 'What a day, Potter—I bet you're dead beat.'

He smiled a little. 'That I am, Staff.'

'And I heard Mr Dale say that you'd done a marvellous job, getting the porters organised so well.'

Potter did his best not to look pleased. 'It's my duty,

Staff,' he added. 'Not but what you haven't done yours and no reward expected, either.'

A true enough statement, but one which proved wrong for once. Philomena was on her way to her midday dinner the next day when a porter caught up with her and handed her a very large box. She was already late for her meal, as were several of her friends with her, but that didn't stop them from pausing long enough to tear off the wrappings, to reveal a handsome box of Fortnum and Mason's chocolates, a sumptuous affair of blue brocade and satin ribbons. There was a note with it and there was an excited chorus of: 'Philly—who's the boy-friend? What a dark horse!' An illusion she was able to dispel when she had read the note.

'Probably you had no tea—perhaps these will help to make up for it. We shan't work you so hard in the practice.' It was signed with the doctor's initials.

'Who cares for romance, anyway?' enquired one of her companions. 'That's a three-pound box, Philly—and what does he mean about the practice?'

They had reached their table and Philly was left to guard the chocolates while the others queued for their dinners and hers too. She wondered when he had found the time to buy them, or perhaps he just ordered them by telephone. It had been kind of him—he was always kind and perhaps a bit crafty this time too, making that allusion to the practice. She hoped he had got her note, and now she would have to write another. She remembered that he was to go to Edinburgh, so her thanks would have to wait. She accepted her plate of stew and urged on by her friends, ate it rapidly; if they were quick, there would be time to make tea and sample the chocolates before they were due back on their wards.

CHAPTER FOUR

IF PHILOMENA had expected the week to drag she found herself very mistaken; days had never flown by so quickly, so that she had very little time in which to think over the doctor's proposal. True, she intended accepting his offer, but there was a great deal more to it than that. A hundred and one details would have to be discussed, her stepmother told, her notice given in, the doctor's airy suggestion that she should learn some Dutch before she left to be gone into. All these were at the back of a mind much too busy to deal with them, so that when he returned at the end of the week and she came face to face with him on the landing outside Men's Surgical, all she could do was to gape at him and say hullo in a feeble sort of way.

His crisp 'Busy?' did nothing to help. She was aware that she didn't look at her best; a concussion case had taken exception to her attempts to feed him and she was on her way home to change her apron, covered with

Horlicks, nicely mingled with the medicine he had thrown at her, her cap crooked and a ladder in her tights where she had slipped against the bed. She frowned quite fiercely at him. 'Yes, as a matter of fact, I am.'

He smiled at her. 'Beastly stuff, Horlicks,' he observed mildly. 'Don't let me keep you.'

Philomena gathered her reeking apron close and flew past him and down the stairs, reflecting that when they met it was always at the wrong moment. And in her room presently, she made herself take her time, not only replacing the offending apron, but re-doing her hair, powdering her unremarkable nose and changing her tights. Mr Dale was just about due for his round, and it seemed likely that Doctor van der Tacx would accompany him.

It was a pity that her efforts were wasted. There was no sign of him when she got back on to the ward, so she accompanied Sister as she escorted Mr Dale round his beds, behaving in an exemplary fashion so that even Sister Brice could find no fault with her, and when he had at last gone, dished out the patients' dinners in her usual serene fashion. But her thoughts were by no means serene. All right, let him walk off like that—perhaps he had thought better of offering her the job, perhaps he had met a far more suitable girl while he had been in Edinburgh—the Royal Infirmary was renowned for the quality of its nurses, and Scottish nurses, she brooded darkly, were bonny girls. She laid a spoonful of carrots beside the boiled potatoes and added stew—he hadn't even asked when she was off duty. She wiped her hands on the towel draped across her clean apron and wondered if he had left a letter for her.

Despising herself for being weak, she actually went along to the letter rack and looked, and of course there was nothing there. She ate her dinner in a morose frame of mind so unlike her usual self that several of her closest friends wanted to know if she were sickening for something.

She had an afternoon off because Sister Brice, disregarding the recommendations of those superior to her, wished to be off duty that evening while at the same time avoiding doing too much work in the morning, so Philomena had gone on duty at seven-thirty until her dinner and was to go back at five o'clock. It was an off-duty which had been frowned upon for some time now and used only when really necessary, but Sister Brice had been at Faith's a long time now and was a law unto herself. Philomena, muttering darkly, flounced out of the dining room and began the journey over to the nurses' home, trying to make up her mind whether it was worth changing to go out, or choose the easier course and just sit and read.

The choice was made for her; stationed strategically at the door of the nurses' home was Doctor van der Tacx, not exactly lying in wait, for he was reading *The Times* as he lounged against the door and gave no sign of having seen her until she was almost on top of him, when he folded his newspaper neatly, put out a long arm to arrest her progress and remarked placidly: 'There you are! What a wretched off-duty you have, but better than nothing, I suppose. Slip into something comfortable and we'll go out.'

She found her voice. 'I didn't know...' she began, and then: 'I was going to have a quiet afternoon.'

His eyes twinkled down at her. 'My dear Philomena, have you ever known me anything but quiet?' He glanced at his wrist. 'Ten minutes? We can walk in a park and have tea and discuss the details.'

It annoyed her that he had taken it for granted that she was going to take the job; after all, she had said that she would think about it.

'There's a great deal I want to know,' she told him severely.

His instant: 'But of course, you have an inquisitive nature and naturally you're brimming over with questions—women always are,' rather took the wind out of her sails. While she was still thinking of a suitable answer he opened the door and ushered her inside. 'Ten minutes,' he reiterated.

It was ridiculous, she told herself as she shed her uniform and got into her new Jaeger short jacket and matching skirt and paused to thank heaven that she had only that week bought a silky sweater in exactly the same shade of green. She tied back her hair, made up her face, thrust her feet into brown calf shoes, found their matching handbag and tore downstairs.

'And where are you going, Philly?' asked Shirley Dawes, the acknowledged beauty of the hospital and unfortunately aware of it.

Philomena paused briefly. 'I haven't the least idea,' she said a little breathlessly, 'but wherever it is, I'm late.'

It was satisfactory to see Shirley's expression. She would have liked to have told her who was waiting for her downstairs, but ten to one the girl would find some way of getting there first.

The doctor hadn't moved. 'You're punctual,' he informed her mildly, 'a splendid augury for your new job.'

She bounced to a halt beside him. 'You're taking a lot for granted,' she said sharply. 'I haven't said I'd take the job.'

'But you're going to, aren't you, Philly?' He sounded so certain that she found herself saying simply:

'Yes, I am.'

'We'll take a taxi to Regent's Park. It's the nearest, I believe. There's a place close by where we can have tea.'

They were walking across the yard which separated the nurses' home from the hospital. 'I'm on at five o'clock,' Philomena told him.

'Yes, I know—there's plenty of time.' He saw her look of enquiry. 'I rang the ward and asked Sister Brice.

I asked her to tell you that I would be waiting for you—you didn't get the message?'

Philomena's faint ill-humour melted away. 'No...I—I expect she was busy and forgot...'

He pushed open the swing doors at the entrance and stood aside to let her pass him. 'Loyalty,' he commented, 'that's another thing in your favour. I can see that you're going to be a valuable addition to our staff.'

He hailed a taxi and popped her in, talking about nothing much until they were in the park, walking towards Queen Mary's Garden. 'Now, let us get down to ways and means. Will you give in your notice tomorrow morning?—let me see, that means that you will be free at the end of May. Do you feel up to driving yourself over? I will make arrangements for the journey and send you written directions in good time. You can go straight to the clinic in Ommen...someone will be there to take you on to Theo's house and settle you into Ellie's lodgings. We pay rather higher salaries in Holland,' he mentioned a sum well above the pay packet she received from Faith's, 'but the hours are different, of course. Eight o'clock surgery on weekdays, lasting until well after ten o'clock, sometimes later, clinics every afternoon—babies, post and prenatal, ear nose and throat, eyes—we deal with them all, sending on those who need specialised treatment or hospital. Evening surgery again at six o'clock, and that lasts until eight o'clock at least. No clinic on Saturday, but a morning surgery. You'll be free half day Saturday and all Sunday, but one in four you'll be on call for emergencies. We hope to arrange for a part-time nurse to take over one afternoon in the week so that you will have time to shop and so on.' He stopped and looked down at her. 'Quite a programme, isn't it? Still feel like tackling it?'

'Yes,' said Philomena.

'Good. We don't all work in the same place at once, of course—there are always two of us at the clinic, though, but you will be expected to go wherever you're needed most. If Theo has a measles outbreak in Ommen you'll spend most of your time there; if I get whooping cough in Vilsteren you'll give me a helping hand.'

'Yes,' said Philomena again. She had seldom encountered whooping cough, but now she found herself quite looking forward to a possible epidemic of it; Walle would be nice to work for.

They had reached Queen Mary's Garden, pleasant enough in the spring sunshine although it was still chilly weather, and they began to walk briskly along its paths. 'Any questions?' asked the doctor.

'Well, supposing I don't suit—or supposing I find I can't cope?'

'We'll call the whole thing off, of course. Reasonable notice on either side, and no ill-feelings, though I don't expect that will happen.' He stopped suddenly and turned her round to face him. 'Do you?'

'No, I don't.' She felt surprisingly sure of that. 'What about learning Dutch?'

He smiled a little. 'Well, you'll be able to learn the basics in a month, provided you're prepared to work hard at it. I know a Dutchwoman living here—Kensington, Addison Crescent; she works at the Embassy and I'm sure she would give you lessons. I'll fix it for you and ask her to telephone you. We'll pay, of course—after all, you're learning the language to oblige us.' He took her arm. 'That's settled, then. Let's have tea, there's a café in Prince Albert Road.'

Busy in the ward that evening, Philomena found time to reflect that everything had been arranged with astonishing ease. Even if she had wanted to draw back now it would be difficult—but she didn't, she was looking forward to going to Holland and working there, and she was, a small voice at the back of her head reminded her, looking forward to seeing the doctor again and very much more often, too. She went off duty feeling as though her day was complete, although it wasn't quite. During supper she was called to the telephone to find that Mevrouw Kring was anxious to find out if she could start her lessons the very next day. They spent a busy five minutes arranging times to suit them both and rang off in a spirit of promising goodwill. Forgetful of the rest of her supper, Philomena rambled across the yard to her room and got into her dressing gown. Her friends, coming to see what had happened to her ten minutes later, found her bowed over her writing pad, so absorbed that she didn't so much as lift her head.

'Philly, your supper—you forgot it,' and: 'Philly, what are you doing?'

She looked up at that. 'Supper?' she wanted to know. 'I forgot. I'm writing out my notice.'

Her room was bulging with various friends and acquaintances by now, and a chorus of protests deafened her. Indeed, no one believed her until she showed them what she had written. It was Jenny who declared: 'She means it! Philly, explain—here, I'll put the kettle on and you can tell us over a cup of tea.' She paused at the door. 'I say, you're not getting married, are you?'

Philomena giggled. 'Of course I am—he's a millionaire and has six cars and three houses and—and a yacht…'

There was a shriek of laughter. 'Don't be daft' said a voice from the back. It hadn't been said unkindly, but Philomena sighed silently all the same; it was a great drawback being plain…'I've got a job in Holland,' she said cheerfully, 'working for a country town partnership. They want me to go in a month's time. I thought it might be fun.'

'But your Sister's post…you can't speak Dutch…it's so far away,' and: 'Whatever made you do it, Philly?'

She ignored the last question. 'There's nothing for a year at least, and I'm going to take Dutch lessons—it's all arranged. I get the same salary—a little more, actually.'

'What will your family say?' asked Jenny.

Philomena got off the bed and put her mug down on the dressing table. 'Oh, lord, I quite forgot to telephone! I'll go now—keep some tea for me.'

Her stepmother thought it might be rather fun, although she didn't want to know a great deal about it—indeed, she didn't ask with whom Philomena was going to work or where, and when Philomena started to tell her she said with careless affection: 'Not now, darling—I'm just in from a simply appalling dinner party, so boring, and that ghastly Mrs Lovell was there and simply dominated the conversation. You'll be home before you go, I expect? We'll have a nice chat then. Do you see anything of that nice Walle van der Tacx?'

'Well, actually...' began Philomena, and was interrupted with:

'Of course he goes on the wards sometimes, I suppose, but that's hardly social, is it? One can hardly expect...I simply must ring off, darling Philly, I'm dog tired—such an evening!'

Philomena went back to her room trying not to feel let down; after all, her stepmother had never taken much interest in her work at the hospital, and it was hardly likely that she should change. Something of her feelings must have been reflected in her face as she joined her friends, for no one said much, a few comments about surprising her family as she was pressed to have more tea, and that was all before they plunged into the more interesting aspects of her future—clothes, for instance, and did people in Holland live any differently from people in England? 'And are they all as handsome as that gorgeous type who strides round with Mr Dale?' someone wanted to know. 'Keep a weather eye open for him, Philly.' And Jenny added kindly: 'You never know, perhaps you'll meet him.'

'I daresay I shall,' said Philomena calmly. 'He's one of the partners in the practice I'm going to work for.'

And after that the hurt from her stepmother's lack of interest was quite swamped in the excited interest of her friends. 'Philly, you dark horse...how about having me over for a weekend? How did you manage it?' And from Shirley Dawes, who had just put her head round the door to see what all the noise was about: 'So that's where you were going all dolled up. I should have thought...' her gaze slid over the various pretty and not quite so pretty faces and returned to Philomena. 'Whatever does he see in you, Philomena?'

Philomena itched to slap the lovely face. 'He sees a hard-working girl who won't want to go out every evening, has no immediate prospect of getting married and with no nonsense about her.' Her voice was almost placid and she grinned as she spoke, so that Shirley, discomfited, stood for a moment in the doorway, just staring, and as no one offered her tea, she went away.

'Cat!' declared Jenny. 'Clever old you to think up

that bit about not going out in the evening, and no matrimonial prospects.'

'I didn't,' said Philomena flatly. 'That was exactly what he did say.'

She gave in her notice the next morning, and although her superior pointed out that she was behaving in a rather rash fashion, especially with promotion ahead of her, she politely refused to reconsider her decision and skipped off through the hospital back to the ward to break the news to Sister Brice.

The month went quickly. What with her Dutch lessons, a number of shopping expeditions and a variety of farewell parties given by her various friends, Philomena had little time to wonder if she was doing the right thing, and when she went home to say goodbye to her stepmother and Chloe and Miriam, they made so light of the matter that her vague doubts were quite put at rest. It was only as she was on the point of leaving that her stepmother asked her where exactly she would be working: 'And you'd better give me the name of the doctor, I suppose, and your telephone number—you know how we hate writing letters, darling—you can ring us up when you feel like it.'

'Ommen,' said Philomena, 'that's the name of the town. I'm to work for a partnership of doctors as their surgery nurse—you've met one of them: Doctor van der Tacx.'

There was a little silence while the three of them stared at her.

Then: 'Philly, however did you manage it?' asked Chloe.

'Well, I didn't. They want a hard-working girl who doesn't hanker for the bright lights and he—he seemed to think I filled the bill.'

'He's quite right,' agreed her stepmother kindly. 'I'm sure you'll be exactly what they expect.'

Philomena didn't answer; she remembered her resolve, she remembered too the case full of new clothes she had purchased with such care and the new make-up she had chosen. They would help to turn her into a different girl, someone the doctor might look at twice and realise that there were other aspects of her besides being hard-working and loyal and punctual. She said goodbye and got into the Mini and drove back to London, a little scared of the traffic when she reached the city, but determined to overcome her fear. The kind of girl she intended to become was a super driver...

The same determination had driven her on to work at her Dutch lessons. Her teacher was a reserved, middle-aged woman who had, however, unbent considerably when she discovered that Philomena really wanted to speak Dutch and understand it too. A month wasn't nearly long enough, of course, but at least at the end of that time Philomena had learned the basics of that language; her accent might not be all that her teacher could wish, but she had mastered a little simple reading and could understand a good deal of what was said to her.

She set out for Holland a few days later, after a splendid send-off by her friends at the hospital, a homily from Sister Brice about remembering that she was now a trained nurse and should always act accordingly, and the good wishes of the patients on the ward. They had clubbed together to give her a present, a box of beautifully embroidered handkerchiefs, and there had been a card too, signed with their names. Philomena packed it with her new clothes, looking upon it as a kind of good luck symbol.

She had arranged to go from Sheerness, because that way, Doctor van der Tacx had assured her in a business-like letter confirming her appointment, would be easier for her, avoiding Rotterdam and the busy heart of the country. She had pored over a map for hours, learning the route by heart, trying to reckon how long the journey would take. But at least she would have the whole day in which to travel, as the ferry got in early in the morning and she could breakfast on it before she landed.

She managed the trip to Sheerness well enough, drove the Mini on board and went to her cabin; she had had supper before she had left London and a night's rest seemed a good idea. She found the cafeteria, had a cup of coffee and then got ready for the night, not expecting to sleep very much. It was a calm night and the idea of feeling queasy hadn't entered her head, but she felt excited and just a little apprehensive about the journey the next day. She made herself comfortable in her bunk, turned out the light and marshalled her thoughts, and that was as far as she got; the next thing she knew, the stewardess was at the door with her breakfast.

Philomena edged the Mini off the ferry into a torrent of rain, made worse because the horizon was so wide; from all points of the compass the sky was a uniform grey and even darker in the direction which she was to take, an unwelcome surprise after the fine night. She drove down the narrow rutted lane which led from the dock to the main road and turned on to the motorway. The rain was like a steel curtain and she could see very little, but she didn't dare to stop, what with keeping to the right side of the road and looking where she was going, but after a little while her panic subsided and she urged the little car to a higher speed, hoping that the weather would improve. At least the motorway stretched before her, straight ahead and with no S bends and few trees to obscure her view.

She drove steadily on, Bergen-op-Zoom, Rozendaal, Breda... She stopped here for coffee while the rain still teemed down, turning everything in sight into a grey monotone, and then pressed steadily on to Tilburg and then Nijmegen and Arnhem. She took a wrong turning in the city and, hungry by now, parked the car and had a meal, and after that it was easier. For one thing, she reckoned that she hadn't much over sixty miles to go and although it was still raining the downpour had

dwindled into a steady drizzle. She travelled across a
dripping Veluwe to Appeldoorn, by-passed the city and
took the road to Raalte as the doctor had instructed her.

She was off the motorway now, with no large towns
close by and few villages. The country around her was
flat and rather dull in the rain, and she was getting tired.
Raalte, when she reached it, looked inviting—she
stopped at a café and asked for tea, to be offered a glass
of boiling water with a tea bag in it, and no milk. But
the short rest was pleasant and the tea, while not quite
as she had expected, was refreshing. She began the last
leg of her journey in fine spirits, occupying herself in
wondering what the doctor would say to her when they
met. Surely her new Jaeger trouser suit, the new make-
up and her hair tied back and hanging its shining length
down her back would have transformed her sufficiently
for him to make some comment. She found herself
looking forward to their meeting.

A waste of time; he wasn't there. Philomena found the
clinic without much trouble. Ommen was a small town
and the clinic, close to the church, could scarcely be
missed, for the church stood in the centre of the little
place, in a cobbled square, and it only needed a slow
drive round it for her to discover the narrow lane which
had been described to her. The clinic was still open; she
parked the Mini tidily on the edge of the square and
walked the short distance down the lane and poked her
head into the clinic's door. It was empty, the last of the

patients gone no doubt, but she could hear voices behind a closed door across the waiting room and she went and knocked on it, pleased at the idea of seeing the doctor once more. A girl opened the door, a big fair girl with bright blue eyes and a pleasant face. She said at once: 'Miss Parsons,' and beamed a welcome as she ushered her in. The room was a small surgery, rather crammed with equipment and with a large desk behind which sat a man who got to his feet as she went in. He was a youngish man, of middle height and heavily built, with a great quantity of dark hair and a magnificent beard and moustache. He gripped her hand and shook it vigorously.

'Theo de Klein,' he smiled at her. 'And you are Miss Philomena Parsons. We are delighted to welcome you, although it is to be regretted that the weather has treated you so badly. Not a good journey from Vlissingen, I should imagine.'

Philomena, relieved to have arrived and at the same time disappointed that Walle van der Tacx wasn't there, smiled a little shyly at him. 'It seemed a long way, but I only got lost twice and the rain was rather awful. It's nice to have got here, though.'

He nodded. 'Splendid, splendid. We will go to Mevrouw de Winter's house where Ellie, our nurse, lodged and you shall see your new home. This is Corrie who works for us part-time. We have finished for the day and we will go now.'

The three of them left the clinic five minutes later and when Philomena turned towards the Mini, Doctor de Klein said: 'No, no, your little car may stay there for a time; there is room in my garage for it and presently you shall drive it there; Mevrouw de Winter lives only a few steps away. We will say goodnight to Corrie, who lives on the other side of the town.'

Goodnights said, the two of them crossed the lane, walked a few yards down its cobbled length and turned into another even narrower lane, one side abutting on to the church, the other lined with a row of small very neat houses. At the second of these Doctor de Klein stopped, banged the knocker and then opened the door, calling something as he did so. The hall was narrow and rather dark with a narrow, steep staircase directly in front of them and a door at the side through which now emerged an elderly lady. She was a large woman, very stout and dressed in black, and when she spoke her voice was loud and rather breathless, but her face was kind and she was smiling broadly.

'Mevrouw de Winter,' introduced Doctor de Klein, and Philomena, glad of the opportunity of airing her hard-learned Dutch, said: '*Aangenaam, mevrouw,*' which was a mistake, for that good lady, supposing her to be fluent in that language, broke into a torrent of words, only a very few of which Philomena understood. It was fortunate that the doctor intervened hastily and

explained, making Mevrouw de Winter laugh heartily
as she led the way into the sitting room.

'Your room is upstairs,' explained Doctor de Klein,
'but Mevrouw de Winter would like you to come here for
your meals. There is an electric fire in your room, but you
are welcome to use this one as often as you like. There
is another room, but that is the best parlour and never
used. Now I will wait here while you see your room and
then we will go together and get your luggage—your car
will be quite safe if you move it in front of the clinic. You
will give my wife and me the pleasure of your company
at supper this evening? I will walk round for you in an
hour or so and we can go in your car to my house where
there is room for you to garage the car.'

Philomena thanked him and followed her landlady
from the room and up the stairs. The landing was so
small that there was barely space in which to turn round
and there were only two doors, one of which Mevrouw
de Winter opened, revealing a surprisingly comfortably
furnished room, its small window overlooking the street
below, the narrow bed pushed up against one wall to
make room for the easy chair and table. There were
shelves along the walls and a number of pictures and in
one corner a washbasin. Philomena smiled and nodded,
then followed Mevrouw de Winter downstairs again
and went along to get her luggage and move the Mini.
She spent the next hour settling in, setting her own
small odds and ends around the room which was to be

her home for the foreseeable future, and then tidying herself ready for her supper date. It was while they were walking to the car that she asked diffidently: 'Doctor van der Tacx—he—he doesn't live here?'

Her companion shot her a sidelong glance. 'I quite forgot to tell you—he is away. He is frequently away, for he lectures a good deal, you know. I am not certain when he will be back. I understand that you saw something of each other in London?'

Philomena murmured that yes, they had, and made some remark about the town, which as far as she could see was charming. It was built on either side of a river, with a handsome bridge spanning it, and now that she had the leisure to look around her, she could see that it was a very small town indeed, its heart packed tightly round the church, while larger villas were spread out towards the wooded country around. They crossed the bridge and at her companion's direction, she turned the car off the main road on its other side into a narrow lane with houses scattered on either side of it. Doctor de Klein lived in a fair-sized house not too far from the road and, obedient to his instructions, Philomena drove down its short drive and pulled up at the front door, which was opened so smartly that she suspected that some had been on the lookout for them. As indeed they had; a child of seven or eight—a small girl with flaxen hair and blue eyes, who ran to meet them as they got out of the car.

'Our youngest daughter,' explained Doctor de Klein.

'We have three, and two boys. This is Marieke.' He stooped to kiss the little girl and then waited while Philomena shook hands with her, and then led the way indoors.

The house was pleasant; comfortably furnished with thick carpets on the floors and several antique chests and cupboards against the walls. They went straight to the sitting room, large and high-ceilinged, where the doctor's wife was waiting for them; a small, bustling little woman, still young and pretty, who greeted Philomena in English and made her feel at home immediately. The rest of the children came in shortly afterwards and they all sat down to dinner, and afterwards Philomena stayed for an hour or two before Doctor de Klein walked her back to her lodgings again. It had been an exciting day, she told herself sleepily as she got ready for bed, and a very long one; tomorrow would be even more exciting, she supposed, and the sooner she went to sleep the better she would be able to face her new job.

It wasn't as bad as she had expected. For one thing, she found to her surprise that her Dutch lessons had been worthwhile, for once she had got over her initial shyness at speaking a foreign language, the basic sentences she had learned to speak and understand stood her in good stead, and as for the work, it was so like a GP's surgery at home that she quite forgot she wasn't in her own country. Besides, Corrie was there to show where everything was and answer the telephone when the receptionist was busy, although as Doctor de Klein pointed out, that would be only for a few days, then she would return to her usual hours, relieving Philomena. But now, with the two of them, the surgery work went smoothly, and as Corrie pointed out, there weren't a great many patients; a mixed bag of small boys with cuts that needed a stitch or two, harassed mothers with small babies, and a sprinkling of elderly men and women with bad chests and varicose veins and rheumatism.

'Wait until this afternoon,' warned Corrie, watching Philomena expertly undressing a small baby. 'It is the children's clinic—Doctor Herman Stanversen will be here too and it will be very busy. Doctor van der Tacx is away and that is a good thing, for when he is here as well there is no moment of peace. He works hard, and we must work hard also to keep up with him. You have met him, I think? He is so handsome,' Corrie rolled her eyes ceilingwards, 'but it is of no use for us to wish for his interest.'

Philomena wrapped the baby neatly into a small blanket. 'Why not?'

'There is a girl—an adopted cousin, I think. She is young and so very pretty. We see her at *Oude en Nieuw*—your New Year—when there is a party at his house, and it is supposed that he will marry her some day.' She added slowly: 'I do not like her.'

Philomena was shocked to find that although she had never set eyes on the girl, she didn't like her either. She said diplomatically: 'Perhaps she's nice when you know her.'

Corrie laughed, whipped out her pen and began to fill in an X-ray form. 'Know her? There is little chance. We are—how do you say?—dust under her feet.'

There was no time to talk again. Philomena bore the baby away to be inspected by Doctor Stanversen, whom she liked; he was tall and very thin, his hair already sparse on top of his earnest face. He had a kind smile, though, and had invited her to go to his home and meet his wife. 'We live at Dalfsen, you know that, I expect— a small village not far from Ommen. I have a surgery there, of course, in fact we all three have a surgery in our homes, but mostly we work here in the clinic. It is convenient for most of our patients, as the practice is widespread! Doctor van der Tacx, whom you already know, is often away, for he is the senior and something of an authority on anaesthetics—indeed, he lectures frequently, but he comes several times a week when he is home. He has a great many patients.'

To all of which Philomena lent an interested ear.

She went back to Mevrouw de Winter for her midday meal; bread and butter and sausage and cheese and a salad, and all the coffee she could drink, while her landlady stood in the kitchen peeling potatoes and talking, patiently repeating her remarks until Philomena understood at least part of them, standing at the open doorway between the two little rooms. Philomena would have liked to linger for a while, but the clinic started at half past one. She carried her dishes into the kitchen, wished Mevrouw de Winter a cheerful '*Dag*' and crossed the road to the clinic. It was a lovely afternoon, although chilly, and she wished momentarily that she was free to spend an hour or two exploring Ommen; she still had to discuss her hours with Doctor de Klein, but that could be done later when he was free. She opened the clinic door on to a full waiting room, and hurried across to the little room at the back where Corrie would be arranging the patients' notes.

The afternoon went so fast, Philomena was surprised when the last patient, a small boy with a suspected mastoid, had been examined, dosed with antibiotic and despatched to the hospital at Zwolle. She tidied up with Corrie and tried not to look surprised when Doctor de Klein told her that his evening session would start at half past six at his house and could she find her own way there?

'You will have your evening meal first,' he pointed out, 'and the surgery lasts only an hour or so. Tomorrow we will speak of your free time—today has been an exception, but Doctor van der Tacx thought it advisable that you should get into the routine as quickly as possible.'

So she hurried back to her lodgings once more, ate Mevrouw de Winter's meat balls and red cabbage with a healthy appetite, and walked round to the doctor's house. The surgery wasn't busy, she was home again within two hours and for a moment she was tempted to go for a walk in the town, but she was tired now and there would be other days when she was free. She drank more of Mevrouw de Winter's excellent coffee and took herself off to bed.

CHAPTER FIVE

PHILOMENA HAD BEEN in Ommen for five days and was tidying the clinic after afternoon session and looking forward to her tea and a free evening, when Walle van der Tacx walked in. His, 'There you are,' was hardly the greeting she had expected, but he didn't seem to notice her rather tart: 'As you see, Doctor van der Tacx.'

He was wearing tweeds, expensive and not so new, and he had his hands in his pockets, a habit she deplored. He looked at her now and her heart sank a little because it was quite obvious to her that he didn't see the new hairstyle or the delicate make-up, although that was perhaps expecting a little too much; her new image didn't have much chance in uniform...

'Measles,' he observed. 'There's an outbreak in the village—all children from the *kleuterschool* and if we're not careful, all their little brothers and sisters will be down with it too. I've arranged a clinic for this evening and we can get them inoculated. I shall need you, of course.' He glanced round him. 'You've finished here?'

It was on the tip of her tongue to tell him that she hadn't only finished there, she had finished for the day too, that she was free that evening after a busy day's work, but instead she said matter-of-factly: 'You want to go at once? Give me a couple of minutes while I lock up.'

She did so rapidly, her mind longingly on her tea. In the car presently she asked: 'Your village—Vilsteren, isn't it?'

'Yes.' He had sent the Khamsin shooting down a country road, away from the little town. The road was pretty, the trees on either side already green, the meadows beyond them lush in the late afternoon sun. It ran parallel with the river, and Philomena could see the water from time to time. The journey was short, which was perhaps why the doctor didn't bother to talk. Only as he stopped in the centre of the village did he remark: 'In the schoolhouse—it shouldn't take too long.'

Philomena spared a moment to look around her. Vilsteren was a delightful little place, enwrapped in trees and with a smart country inn in the curve of the road. It looked nice, she thought, and obviously a good class restaurant—probably the people of Ommen came out to it on special occasions. She followed the doctor across the narrow road and in at the schoolhouse door, to find one of its two classrooms already filled with mothers and small children. Apparently it was to be used as a waiting room while the doctor used the second room. Philomena hung her cloak behind the door, said *'Goeden avond'* to the room in general and rolled up her sleeves.

The doctor had been over optimistic, though—it took longer than either of them had expected. For one thing, Philomena was still a little slow at getting names right on the forms and for another several of the children took strong exception to having an injection; no amount of cajoling could make them think otherwise. Philomena resorted to guile finally, offering the sweets she had hastily bought from the obliging village shop, specially opened for the emergency, to each protesting child, finally taking off jackets and woollies and rolling up sleeves so that the surprisingly patient doctor could pop in his needle. It was evening by the time the last snivelling child had been hurried away home to bed and Philomena, tidying up briskly, her hungry mouth full of toffee, heaved a sigh of relief. But she was careful to show a placid face to her companion; he had remained calm and good-natured with his small patients, but she had the feeling that he was annoyed about something. Herself, perhaps; she had been a little slow with names, although she hadn't faltered once with the actual work. She put on her cape and waited by the door while he shut and locked it and then went with him to the car. As they went past the restaurant she just prevented herself in time from openly sniffing at the delicious smells coming from its open door.

They were back in Ommen before Doctor van der Tacx spoke and then it was only to thank her for her help, but when he stopped close by Mevrouw de Winter's small house he switched off the engine and got out to open her door. 'It took longer than I had imagined,' he observed.

She looked up at him and smiled a little. 'Yes, but there's still plenty of evening left.'

He didn't smile. 'I had a date—with Tritia, my cousin—my adopted cousin. She has lived with one of my aunts for years and we see a good deal of her. She will be very disappointed.'

'And you're disappointed too,' observed Philomena.

'Yes.'

'There will be other evenings,' she pointed out kindly. 'I'm sorry your evening has been spoilt.' And hers too, she added silently; supper and bed and perhaps half an hour's difficult conversation with her landlady; not exactly what she had planned. She said goodnight and went indoors, to be met by Mevrouw de Winter's gentle scolding because her supper had been ready for more than an hour.

She was changing a dressing on an old lady's varicose ulcer the next morning when Doctor van der Tacx put his head round the door. He wished the old lady a good day before turning to Philomena. 'I owe you an apology,' he said, 'I didn't stop to think about you—the least I could have done was to have given you a meal to make up for your lost free time.'

She eyed him steadily. 'But I wasn't doing anything special, you must have realised that,' and at his sudden sharp glance: 'I've only been here six days, you know, hardly time to get to know anyone.'

She fastened her bandage and began to roll up the old lady's stocking. She had taken great pains with her hair that morning and the new make-up, now that she had got expert with it, must surely have improved her mediocre looks. She didn't look at him but smiled at her patient, told her haltingly to return in a week and led her to the door. The doctor opened it wider and stood on one side and then, when Philomena would have gone through too, closed it. 'I've been thinking about that,' he told her. 'Would you like to spend Sunday at my home? My mother would like to meet you.'

Regret welled up so strongly that she had a job to answer him. 'How kind of you, but I'm spending the weekend with Doctor and Mevrouw Stanversen—but please thank your mother—I hope she'll ask me again.'

'She will be away for a week or so,' he answered carelessly. 'When she returns, perhaps. You're settling down, I hope? You're comfortable with Mevrouw de Winter?'

'I'm very happy, thank you, Doctor.' She was getting another dressing tray ready.

'No regrets?' he persisted.

'None. Ommen seems a delightful place and the country round it is charming.'

'What do you do with your evenings? Are you not lonely? Don't you miss the cinema and dinner out or the theatre?'

'I didn't go out a great deal,' she told him drily, 'so I don't miss any of them, and I've only had two evenings so far.' She longed to remind him that she had been given the job in the first place because she was a sensible girl not given to gallivanting every night of the week, but she didn't. 'That's Doctor de Klein's bell,' she informed him. 'He's ready for his next patient.'

He opened the door at once. She was almost through it when he said to surprise her: 'You've done something to your hair—it looks very pretty.'

She was too busy to analyse her feelings at his remark, but the glow of satisfaction was reflected in her face so that Doctor de Klein, glancing up as she ushered the next patient in, decided that he had been mistaken and that she wasn't such a very plain girl, after all.

Doctor Stanversen had suggested that he should fetch her on Saturday afternoon and drive her to Dalfsen, but Philomena had asked if she might drive herself in the Mini; the more experience she had on the Dutch roads, the better; later she would explore further afield. So on Saturday afternoon she set out under a bright May sky, wearing one of her new outfits; green slacks and a

knitted cotton top in white and green, with a matching
cardigan if it should get chilly. She had prudently put
her raincoat in the car too, and packed a dress in her
overnight bag just in case the Stanversens liked to be
formal in the evening. The road took her through
Vilsteren again, and once through the village it became
even prettier with great trees arched overhead and
expensive-looking bungalows and small villas tucked
away behind well laid out gardens. She wondered if
Doctor van der Tacx lived in one of them. She could ask
the Stanversens, of course, but that would look nosey;
she would have to wait until he invited her again to his
home. Perhaps he wouldn't; perhaps he had been
making a conventional friendly gesture in case she was
lonely.

The road curved gently and she slowed to admire a
castle standing well back from the road, the river
glinting behind it, trees grouped around its park,
through which the drive ran as straight as a ruler to
widen into a circle of gravel around its walls. Its
windows were long and narrow and their green and
white painted shutters showed up gaily against the
brickwork. Philomena put her neatly shod foot down on
the accelerator. 'And very nice too,' she told herself
aloud, 'though I suppose it's an agricultural college or
something equally unromantic!'

Dalfsen, when she reached it, was charming. It lay
on the further side of the river and she had to cross a

bridge to reach its church and cluster of houses, and it
didn't prove difficult to find Doctor Stanversen's house.
It stood back from the village square, solid and large-
windowed, its garden, filled with spring flowers, hedged
by an iron railing. Philomena drove the Mini up its
short drive and was getting out when the door opened
and her host came to meet her. He looked thinner and
taller than ever in an elderly tweed jacket and even
older slacks, accounted for by the garden shears he was
holding in one hand. His greeting was pleasantly
friendly as he put down the shears, got her bag from the
car and led her indoors, letting out a bellow for his wife
as he did so. All the doors in the hall seemed to open at
once; his wife, a big woman with a long, serious face;
several children, and an elderly woman with the coffee
tray all converged on them.

'Tina, my wife,' said Doctor Stanversen, and
Philomena discovered that the serious face could smile
with such charm that its owner became at once a nice-
looking young woman, 'the children...' There were
four of them, two boys in their early teens and two
girls, one still very small. 'And Lien, who looks after
us all.' The elderly woman nodded and smiled and continued on her way with the tray, and they all followed
her into a large, airy room, well furnished with big,
comfortable chairs and several rather splendid antique
cupboards and tables. They sat in a wide circle and
Philomena was relieved to find that Mevrouw

Stanversen spoke English too, as indeed did the two boys and the elder girl.

'You drink tea,' observed her hostess, 'do you not? At four o'clock we will all drink tea, but now I hope that you do not mind coffee?'

Philomena didn't mind at all; the coffee was good, hot and creamy and fragrant. They lingered over it until Mevrouw Stanversen offered to show her her room and they went upstairs, the two girls with them.

They had given her a dear little room, its high window overlooking the village square and beyond, the river and the bridge she had crossed. The three of them sat down and watched her unpack her case and then escorted her downstairs again.

'You would like to go into the garden?' her hostess wanted to know. 'We are busy planting, ready for the summer.'

They found the doctor there, digging in a wide herbaceous border which ran the length of the ground behind the house; the two boys were busy too, Philomena rightly deduced that her help might be welcomed, and presently found herself, a sacking apron over her smart jersey and slacks, heavy gardening gloves on her hands, and wooden *klompen* on her feet, wielding a hoe. And enjoying it.

It must have been an hour or more later when they heard a car stop before the house. The children cast down their gardening tools as one man and raced down the garden and out of sight, and Philomena felt a little spirt of excitement; perhaps it was Walle van der Tacx—after all, the three doctors were good friends, so there must be a fair amount of visiting between them—perhaps he would stay for tea.

The man who came round the corner of the house with the children prancing round him wasn't Walle. She had never seen him before, but as he got nearer she could guess who he was: a brother of Doctor Stanversen, a younger, broader version with fair hair and an open, friendly face. He kissed his sister-in-law now, wrung his brother's hand and looked at Philomena. She found herself smiling back at him as they were introduced, his casual friendliness making her feel that she had known him already. They stood talking for a few minutes and then by common consent collected up the spades and forks and hoes and repaired indoors for tea.

Hubert Stanversen was a doctor too, so he told Philomena, working in a Utrecht hospital as a house physician. He had only been qualified for two years, but although he modestly disclaimed any pretensions to brains, his elder brother told her with some pride that he was thought to be outstanding in his work. 'Give him another five or six years, and he'll outstrip the lot of us,' he observed. 'How about taking Philomena for a walk? There's the village to see and it's pretty down by the river. Wear something warm, Philomena—it may be May, but it's cool in the evenings.'

'And there's always a wind blowing,' she declared. 'It doesn't matter which corner I turn, it meets me head on.'

They all laughed and Doctor Stanversen said: 'I have just remembered that you are owed an evening—Walle borrowed you for the measles injections, didn't he? He told me to see that you had a few hours off to make up for it. Doctor de Klein and I will discuss it on Monday and let you know.'

Philomena put down her cup and saucer. 'Oh, please, it doesn't matter at all...I wasn't going to do anything...'

He smiled at her in a fatherly fashion. 'Ah, but Doctor van der Tacx is the boss around here, you know—if he says you are to have time off, then time off you shall have.' He looked across at his wife. 'My dear, what time do you want us to have our dinner this evening?'

Philomena found herself gently urged to fetch her coat and join Hubert for the suggested walk, and indeed, she wasn't loath to go; she had liked him at once and it was pleasant to have someone to talk to—someone of her own age, more or less, someone to laugh and joke with. She hadn't allowed herself to admit it until now, but she had been just a little lonely.

They wandered round the little place and then made their way down to the river, crossed the bridge and walked on down the road which led eventually back to Ommen. They had been strolling along for five minutes

or so when Doctor van der Tacx passed them in the
Khamsin, driving fast, but not so fast that Philomena
didn't have time to see that he had a passenger; a girl with
short fair hair, sitting beside him, laughing up at him. She
acknowledged his casual wave with a wooden nod and
asked, rather too earnestly, what Hubert's chances of
getting a junior registrar's post were, while she wondered
just where Walle lived—not far away, she was sure. Not
that it mattered; despite his invitation, she didn't think it
likely that he would ask her to his home again; he had
done the right thing and she hadn't been free to accept.
She listened to her companion's enthusiastic hopes for
the future while she brooded on the waste of most of her
small nest egg on a lot of new clothes.

When they got back to the house and she was in her
room, tidying herself for dinner, she took a long look
in the small mirror above the wall table; it hadn't only
been a waste of money, it had been a waste, full stop.
No smart clothes or different make-up could disguise
the fact that she had no looks to speak of. She had been
silly to imagine even for a moment that Walle would
notice any difference; he had built up a picture of her—
a sensible girl with no nonsense about her and no
prospect of getting married, that was what he had said,
and that was only another way of saying a plain girl with
no hope of being anything else but a bachelor girl for
the rest of her days. She heaved a sigh, blinked her
green eyes rapidly to prevent the weakness of tears,

arranged her hair with more than usual care, and went downstairs to join everyone else.

Back in the clinic on Monday morning, she thought with pleasure of the remainder of her weekend; it had been fun and everyone had been kind. And Hubert had asked her to go out with him sometime; no time or place, but his invitation had been sincere and she had accepted with a mild pleasure at the idea of seeing more of him. He was a nice boy, but not of course in the least like Walle…

Philomena saw a good deal of Walle during that week; he was in and out of the clinic each day, and now that she was on her own, she was hard put to it to keep pace with all three of the doctors, but she managed, with the secretary and the receptionist helping her out and her Dutch improving almost hourly. But he had little to say to her, and that concerned his patients, and although his manner was as kind as ever he made no attempt to engage her in conversation, indeed, he seemed to her to be withdrawn, so much so that to call him Walle even when the clinic was over was more than she cared to do, so she addressed him as Doctor and he didn't seem to object to that. The friendliness she had been so happy about when they had first met seemed to have gone; perhaps he felt that now she was working for him, they should be more formal, and as for his noticing her new clothes and hair-do, that was hopeless for he never saw her except in her white uniform dress with a cap hiding the carefully dressed hair.

When Hubert telephoned on Friday evening and asked her to go out with him on the Sunday, she agreed at once, stifling a wish that it had been Walle who had invited her. It was vexing that on Saturday morning, while she was clearing away after a short clinic, he should arrive and ask her if she would care to go to lunch with his mother on Sunday. She dropped the pile of towels she was folding on to the table and said with real distress: 'Oh, I'm so sorry, I would have loved to, but Hubert Stanversen asked me out; he's coming for me on Sunday morning.' She watched his face anxiously as she spoke, but there was nothing in it to show her if he was disappointed or put out. His: 'Our fault, we should have asked you sooner, but never mind, you will enjoy yourself with young Hubert,' was carelessly cheerful. 'You're not worked too hard, I hope?'

'No, thank you. I like it very much, it's a change from the wards and I enjoy meeting so many people. Were there any more measles in your village?'

'Four more cases from the *kleurterschool*, but none of those we dealt with—although there's time enough for them to develop spots. I hope it's checked. Did you get your free time made up to you?'

'Yes, thank you.' She stood quietly, wishing she could think of something to say while he stood staring down at her, but her head was empty; in a minute he would go, and she would have liked him to have stayed.

'You hear from your family—your sisters?' he asked suddenly.

'Well, no—they don't have much time for letter writing.' That sounded silly, so she added: 'They don't like it anyway. I telephoned my stepmother last week. They—they go out a good deal, especially in the summer.'

He nodded slowly. 'I'm sure they must—such charming girls and so lovely.'

She had no idea what made her say: 'The girl with you in your car last weekend was lovely too.'

He smiled a little and his voice was bland. 'Yes, is she not? That was Tritia, she certainly livens up my rather orderly life.'

She had nothing to say to this and presently he asked gently: 'You enjoy Hubert's company?'

She didn't suppose that he really wanted to know; she answered cautiously: 'He seems very nice.'

Walle leaned back against the desk, his hands in his pockets, as though he had all day in which to gossip. 'He has a very good future, I believe.' His glance fell on the pile of towels Philomena had folded and unfolded and folded again and his eyes held a gleam of amusement. 'Don't let me keep you, Philly—I've some work to do. Enjoy your weekend.'

He sauntered away to his office and closed the door quietly behind him, leaving her to put the towels away without ceremony and wish vaguely that he wouldn't call her Philly; somehow when he did her name didn't sound the same as when anyone else said it.

Hubert arrived soon after breakfast on Sunday,

admired her outfit with suitable warmth, handed her into his Saab, settled himself beside her and asked her where she would like to go. Quite unfairly, this irritated her; she would have liked to have been whisked off for her day out without having a say in the matter, but he looked so earnest that she said at once: 'Well, you know, I don't know Holland at all, almost anywhere will be nice...'

'How about Zwolle and Kampen?'

'I should like that.' She gave him a nice smile as he started the car.

Zwolle was charming, the gardens along its ramparts a sea of spring and early summer flowers. Hubert parked the car and they walked around for half an hour while Philomena admired the pepperpot tower of the Church of our Lady, and the Town Hall and the Sassenpoort gate, while her companion supplied her with the various interesting facts concerning these. He was knowledgeable, but she found him a little too earnest and it was quite a relief when he suggested that they should drive on to Kampen, a town she instantly fell in love with, its lovely old houses and churches spread along the banks of the Ijssel, a wide boulevard separating them from the water. She would have liked to stroll along its length, looking at the tall narrow houses, but Hubert pointed out sensibly enough that there were plenty more houses exactly the same in any town in the country, whereas the Town Hall and a number of the gateways were unique. So she obediently studied them, asking intelligent questions and listening carefully to what he had to say, and was rewarded by coffee in one of the many cafés along the boulevard, while Hubert tried to make up his mind if they should go on to Meppel to the north or turn south to Amersfoort.

He decided finally that Meppel would be the better of the two; they could lunch there and then make their way slowly back via Coeworden. Which they accordingly did, stopping for their meal at a small, pleasant roadside restaurant just outside the town and then going on again. Coeworden, Philomena discovered, wasn't very interesting; it was the centre of the oil drilling industry and although the oil wells were well disguised, she found it a great shame to have spoilt the charming countryside. All the same, she listened to Hubert's explanations and meticulously detailed descriptions of the work; not with all her mind, though. A tiny part of it was wondering what Walle was doing; out with Tritia, she supposed, and most certainly not talking about crude oil and its components.

Hubert, who was interested in oil wells, lingered for some time and it was well past four o'clock when he turned the car's nose towards Ommen once more. They had tea in the hotel on the river bank, watching the gently flowing life of the little town on the opposite bank while the talk, naturally enough, turned to hospital life and Hubert's ambitions for his future. They whiled away a pleasant hour in this way until Philomena reminded him that he had said that he had to be back by early evening to stand in for one of the other house doctors.

They parted outside Mevrouw de Winter's house ten minutes later and Philomena found herself half promising to spend another day with him as soon as he could arrange it. She thanked him for her day, her green eyes smiling at him in a friendly fashion; he was a nice boy and a pleasant companion, if a little pompous at times, but probably, she admitted honestly, she was a dead bore herself sometimes. She stood watching the Saab turn the corner and go round the square, then went indoors, to spend the rest of the evening talking to her landlady in her halting Dutch, before eating her supper and presently going to bed.

Before she slept she wondered sleepily what sort of a day she would have had if she had accepted Walle's invitation. 'At least we wouldn't have talked about oil wells,' she told herself, and registered a vow to get up a little earlier so that she would have the time to apply her make-up to its best possible advantage. Hubert had said that she looked nice; there was no reason why Walle van der Tacx shouldn't think the same…

She had been asleep for just over two hours when the walkie-talkie which stood by her bed roused her. She had been surprised to see it when she had arrived and it had been explained to her that in an emergency it would save time—precious time in a rural practice—as the telephone was in Mevrouw de Winter's sitting room and since she slept lightly and would invariably answer it, there might be a vital lapse of time.

Philomena rolled over in bed and listened to Walle's calm voice. She was to get dressed at once; she would be fetched in ten minutes. There was an emergency— a severe haemorrhage. The woman lived alone in a remote cottage and her small son had got on his bicycle and arrived not five minutes since. She pressed the button as she had been instructed, said 'I'll be ready,' and when there was no reply, got herself out of bed and into sweater and slacks, plaited her hair into a thick golden rope and crept downstairs, her sensible shoes in her hand. She was outside the front door putting them on when the Khamsin drew up almost soundlessly a few yards away.

Walle swung the door open and she got in without speaking. It was the doctor who broke the silence with a cheerful: 'Sorry about this, Philomena, but I shall need help.' He was already racing through the quiet little town and on to the Dalfsen road and then through Vilsteren, to turn off presently down what was little more than a cart track. 'I left the child at home,' the doctor observed. 'He's only nine and terrified—his mother, from his garbled description, is aborting. His father is away, God knows where. She must be five months; we'll get to work on her and then get her to

Zwolle.' He was thinking out loud now. 'Let me see, I saw her almost three months ago and she was well, but rather anaemic—not young any more either.'

He had slowed the car, easing it over the potholes and ridges of dried clay, and turned to look at her in the pale dark of the night. He was in slacks and a sweater too, she noticed, and looked as calm and unruffled as he normally did. His half seen smile warmed her. 'We're almost there. We'll have to walk the last few yards. There's a torch in the pocket beside you—we'll need it. There are only oil lamps and candles.'

She followed him up the narrow neglected path to a stout little door set in the side of a small, dilapidated cottage. There was a faint glimmer of light showing from the window, but no sound. The doctor opened the door, warned Philomena to keep close behind him, and went in. The light came from the open door of a room leading out of the living room they were standing in and he crossed the room, his bag in his hand. The patient lay in bed, pale and unconscious, her face full of grey shadows. The doctor turned back the bedclothes and gave a little grunt. 'Right, let's get a drip up—it's all there in my bag'—he had his stethoscope out and was bending over the woman—'and hand me the…' He didn't need to finish; Philomena had the sphygmomanometer out and was holding it ready. 'It's incomplete,' he went on, 'she'll need surgery.' He read the blood pressure, tossed the case on to the bed and began to clean up the woman's arm so that he could insert a cannula. 'Find something we can hang the bag on to,' he asked Philomena, 'and a couple more candles…'

She found an old-fashioned hat-stand and trundled it in and set it by the bed, then went back for the equally old-fashioned table lamp in the living room. There were matches beside it and she lighted it and carried it through to the bedroom, and that done, quietly did as she was told like the good nurse she was.

Presently the doctor straightened his long back. 'Right—I'm going to take her at once. I'm afraid you'll have to stay and clear up in case the child comes back early in the morning. Take the torch and light the way, will you? We'll have her in front and prop her up with pillows and blankets.'

He scooped the still unconscious woman up and Philomena nipped ahead, opened doors, shining the torch's beam behind her, a snatched-up pillow under one arm. It was amazing how quick one could be in an emergency, she thought, fastening the seat belt round a cocoon of blankets. She nodded briskly at the doctor's: 'I shan't be long,' and stood watching the car's tail lights disappearing down the track. Ommen, she reflected, was eighteen miles from Zwolle and they had come five miles or so of that distance—an hour should see him back again. She went up the little path, telling herself that an hour was no time at all, and there was a fearsome amount of clearing up to do.

It was very quiet now and the night, what was left of it, had clouded over. She felt the first drops of rain on her face as she went into the cottage and shut the door. She was only dimly aware of the noise of the downpour as she worked; there was a great deal to do, and before she could begin she had to hunt round for cloths and brushes and buckets as well as bed linen. There was no hot water, and she quickly decided that to wait for a kettle to boil on the paraffin stove standing on the kitchen table would take too long. She cleaned and scrubbed and tidied until she was satisfied that everything was as near its original state as possible, washed her hands at the sink, and went to sit down, the lamp on the table beside her for company.

The rain had become torrential, its noise drowning any sound as it poured off the roof where the gutters had broken. Philomena listened to it, wishing that Walle would come back. She hadn't bothered with the time, but now she got up and went into the tiny lean-to kitchen and peered at the battered alarm clock on a shelf, her lamp held high. It was turned three o'clock. It would be growing light soon, she told herself sensibly; the rain couldn't go on for ever and at this time of the year the nights were short. And as if in answer to her thought, the rain stopped with uncanny suddenness, leaving a stillness which made her look around uneasily.

She went back to her chair and sat down, making herself study the little room calmly. Her slow gaze took in the shabby furniture, the worn rug, the splintered floor boards, the torn wallpaper on the farther wall…her eyes widened as a dark shape, squeaking nastily, slid along the wainscoting.

Philomena screamed, not loudly, but still a scream, and she screamed again when the doctor spoke from the door.

'My darling girl, what is the matter?'

She rounded on him, her rather sharp little nose quivering with her fright. 'A rat,' she managed, 'there was a rat…'

He was beside her now, a large comforting arm around her shoulders. She went on fiercely: 'You frightened me, creeping in like that!'

'I didn't creep,' he pointed out mildly. 'I expect you didn't hear the car because of the rain. Where's this rat?'

'How should I know?' she told him crossly. 'I expect there are dozens!' Her usually serene voice was shrill with overwrought feelings.

'I should have taken you with me—we could have come back here and cleared up together.'

Philomena sniffed and straightened a little within the circle of his arm. 'That wouldn't have done at all— look at the time we would have wasted, and I'd have been useless at the hospital. I'm sorry I've been silly— it was the rat and all that rain, and then it stopped so suddenly…it was so quiet and then it squeaked…' She stopped because she was getting a little muddled, and anyway Walle didn't want to waste what time there was listening to her moaning about rats. 'Is the woman going to be all right?'

His grip tightened. 'I believe so—very largely due to you, Philly. She was in theatre when I left. I'll telephone when I get back home.' He let her go gently. 'You've done a splendid job here. Do you want me to do anything before we go?'

'Well...' she hesitated, 'I've put everything in to soak, but there's a lot of washing to do.'

'I'll send someone over later on.' His glance swept round the poor little room. 'We must find another home for the poor soul.'

'The boy?' asked Philomena.

'I'll make arrangements for him to lodge in the village until his mother's better.' He took her arm and ushered her out of the cottage, closed the door and led the way down the muddy path to the car, and Philomena, trailing behind him, noticed that the clouds were clearing from a sky already pale with dawn. She got into the car, stifling a yawn, and as the doctor leaned over to fasten her seat belt, he observed: 'Bed for you, my girl; there are still a few hours left.'

She agreed sleepily. 'What a pity that you have to drive me back to Ommen. Now if there was a bike, I could...'

He interrupted her with a chuckle. 'You would go to sleep in the saddle and fall off. Besides, you're not going to Ommen; you're coming home with me.'

CHAPTER SIX

PHILOMENA WAS aware of a variety of feelings; delight at the prospect of bed so close at hand, pleasure at discovering just where Walle lived and vexation that she had no toothbrush or comb, jumbled nicely with instant worry as to how she was to get to the clinic in Ommen by eight o'clock and how simply frightful she was going to look without any make-up. She began: 'Yes, but...' to be hushed by her companion with a: 'Don't fuss, Philly, we're both too tired.'

So she lapsed into silence while he negotiated the lane and then tore along the road, going, she noticed, towards Dalfsen. But not for long. The moon, free of clouds, lighted the road ahead of them and as they took a curve, shone on the castle she had stopped to admire when she had gone to Dalfsen. She admired it now and then caught her breath as the doctor slowed the car, slid between the great open iron gates and started up the drive.

'Do you live here?' asked Philomena hollowly.

'Yes. We'll go straight to the garage if you don't mind and go in through the back—my mother and cousin sleep in the front of the house.'

He swept the car gently round the lovely old building under an archway and into a wide courtyard encircled by outbuildings. The garage took up the whole of one side with three wide doors, one of which slid back as they approached it. There were other cars there, but Philomena was allowed no time to look around her as they got out. A firm hand guided her across the court-yard to a small very solid door set in the wall which the doctor unlocked. It gave on to a narrow passage, lighted dimly, which led to a wide corridor, close-carpeted in crimson and which led in turn to an arched doorway. The doctor threw this door open and ushered Philomena into a vast square hall, with a handsome staircase leading to a gallery above and a magnificent marble floor. Struck dumb by this grandeur, she allowed him to take her hand and lead her across to the staircase, which he proceeded to mount, giving her no time at all in which to examine her surroundings.

The gallery spread away on either side of the stair-case, a number of handsome doors on its inner wall, but these were ignored; Walle turned down a narrow corridor leading away from the gallery, to stop halfway down it and open a door.

'There's a bathroom through that door,' he indicated it as he switched on the lights. 'I'm afraid there's no—

er—nightwear, but you'll find toothbrushes and combs and so on in the wall cupboard.'

He pushed Philomena gently into the centre of the room. 'You'll be called later. Goodnight.'

He had gone, closing the door gently behind him, leaving her with a dozen questions on her tongue and not one of them uttered.

She was tired, but before she undressed she explored the room; a charming apartment, panelled in dark oak and furnished with a small four-poster bed, a tallboy, a handsome pier table with a mirror above it, and a pair of small easy chairs covered in needlework. The floor was carpeted in a dusky pink and the same colour was repeated in the curtains and bedspread, and the whole of one wall was a fitted cupboard. Philomena, much impressed, tried the door next to the bed and found the bathroom and, what was more important, a comb and toothbrush, soap, towels and bath salts. Within minutes she was lying up to her chin in the warm water; there was so little time left for sleep that ten minutes or so couldn't make much difference, and at least she would be clean, with combed hair. She climbed into bed presently and went to sleep immediately.

When she woke, the sun was streaming through the two narrow windows and a stout elderly woman was standing by the bed, carrying a tray. Her '*goeden morgen*' was smilingly said and Philomena, airing her Dutch, did the same and asked the time. When the woman told her ten o'clock she shook her head; obviously she hadn't used the right words, but the woman put down the tray on the bedside table and crossed the room to where a small ormolu clock stood on a wall table and brought it back for Philomena to see. It was indeed that time. 'Oh, lord,' said Philomena, 'I've overslept! Whatever shall I do?' She frowned a little, trying to think of the Dutch for overslept, but as it turned out, it wasn't necessary, because the woman had produced an envelope and handed it to her.

'Go down to the sitting room when you have had your breakfast,' the doctor had written. 'I shall fetch you after the morning surgery.'

She looked up at the woman and smiled, and received a motherly smile in return, reminding her strongly of Molly.

'May I know your name?' she asked in her careful Dutch.

'Ellie, Miss Parsons. You will eat your breakfast now? I will fetch you in an hour.'

Philomena nodded again, understanding her easily enough, and when she had gone, sat up in bed and attacked the coffee and toast and rolls, aware suddenly that she was very hungry.

It seemed a pity not to make full use of such a lovely bathroom; she had another bath, dressed quickly, plaited her well-combed hair into a pigtail once more, deplored her unmade-up face and went to look out of the window.

The gardens below were delightful, full of spring flowers and bright with their colours, and beyond it the park stretched down to the river. 'And very nice too,' observed Philomena, and turned to call 'come in' to Ellie's knock.

The hall in daylight looked even more impressive than it had a few hours earlier, with a huge chandelier hanging from the high ceiling and the dark carved wood of the gallery railing contrasting with the white of the floor. She followed Ellie across the hall towards one of the double doors and when Ellie opened it and stood aside, smiling, went into the room beyond.

The room was of a fair size and furnished most comfortably with a number of sofas and big chairs. There was a circular table in the centre of the room, laden with magazines and books, a small davenport under one window, and a dear little work table besides. There was someone sitting in an upright chair by the table, a slim, elderly woman with white hair severely dressed and wearing a dress of dark blue silky material which fell in soft folds around her. She got up as Philomena stood hesitating at the door and came to meet her across the richly patterned carpet.

'Miss Parsons—my son has told me about you, and I am delighted to welcome you to his house.' She shook hands, her placid, nice-looking face breaking into a smile. 'He tells me that you were of the greatest help to him during the night—that poor woman! One of the

maids has just taken the boy to the village—he has no
family other than his mother, but Walle found someone
who will look after him for the time. Sit down, my dear,
and tell me how you like your work. Ellie will bring
coffee in a moment, there will be plenty of time for you
to drink it before Walle comes for you.'

'I missed the surgery—I feel guilty…'

'No need—you deserved your sleep—Walle appre-
ciated your help, my dear.'

Perhaps, thought Philomena, suddenly remembering, that was why he had called her his darling girl.

The doctor came in presently, kissed his parent
lightly on a proffered cheek, wished Philomena a
cheerful, casual good morning, coupled with the hope
that she had slept well, and sat down to drink his coffee,
and after ten minutes or so of gentle conversation, suggested that they should be thinking of going. But before
Philomena could get to her feet, the door was flung
open and Tritia came in—it had to be Tritia; she had the
same eye-catching beauty as her stepsisters; only hers
was golden, hair like silk, blue eyes and the kind of nose
Philomena had always hankered after… She skimmed
across the room to Walle, flung her arms round his neck
and kissed him with a charming little crow of delight,
then looked over her shoulder at Philomena.

'Who is this plain girl?' she asked in Dutch. 'She is
terrible to look at!'

Philomena, who had worked hard at that language

and understood a good deal of what was said, tried to look as though she hadn't understood a word, but the bleak expression on her face brought a suspicious frown to the doctor's face. 'Take care, Tritia—she knows something of our language, and that was unkind. If you had been up half the night, you would look plain too.' He took her arms from his neck and smiled at Philomena. 'This is Tritia, my adopted cousin.' His blue eyes were watchful. 'Her English is bad, perhaps you had better try some of your Dutch.'

Philomena shook hands with a serene smile which nicely concealed her hurt rage. 'Oh, I'm sure your cousin's English couldn't be worse than my Dutch—words are all right, it's when you come to sentences...'

She saw the frown lift from the doctor's face and the small flicker of dislike in the girl's face. She wondered why. She had no looks, she could only agree there, and the doctor had showed her no more attention than he would have offered a maiden aunt. She was the poorest competition, quite beneath the girl's notice. A little demon at the back of her usually sensible mind prodded her into saying: 'I must look frightfully untidy—I've not had the chance to go to my rooms and change into uniform.' She smiled brilliantly at Tritia and then made her farewells to Mevrouw van der Tacx with an unselfconscious ease which was very much at variance with her appearance, before accompanying the doctor out of the room.

It was sheer chance which caused Ellie to come into

the hall as they were crossing it; she stopped to wish
Philomena goodbye and made some remark about the
brevity of her sleep. 'You will be glad to change your
clothes and attend to your hair and face, miss,' she con-
cluded with the kindly interest of an old and devoted
servant. And Philomena, quite forgetting that she had
just declared that her Dutch was fragmental, answered
her readily enough, making a great many mistakes and
mispronouncing her words most dreadfully, but dem-
onstrating very clearly that she was quite capable of
understanding what was said.

It wasn't until they were the other side of the door
and about to get into the car that the doctor remarked
thoughtfully: 'Your Dutch has improved enormously
during the last five minutes, Philomena.'

She gasped and frowned fiercely at her own stu-
pidity and went a bright pink. 'Well, what would you
have done?' she asked him defiantly.

'Probably the same as you,' he told her coolly. 'Tritia
didn't mean a word of it, you know—she's like a
child...'

Philomena would have liked to have disillusioned him
about that, but she was a kind-hearted girl and quite
without conceit. 'She was right,' she observed quietly, 'I
am plain.'

He eyed her in a thoughtful, leisurely way. 'I believe
I told you once that I liked what I saw, Philly... Now
get into the car like a good girl—there's an enormous
clinic this afternoon.'

They were almost there when he said casually: 'If Hubert can spare you, perhaps you would like to spend the weekend with us? My mother would be delighted.'

Of course she would, reflected Philomena sourly. It would be company for the poor lady, probably left alone while her son and Tritia went off together. She let the bit about Hubert pass; it did her flattened ego good to think that her companion imagined, even for a few minutes, that the young man was interested in her. She said sedately: 'Thank you, that would be delightful.'

'Good, I'll pick you up about half past eleven on Saturday.'

Saturday was the other end of the week, but there was little time to dwell on the possible delights in store for her. She changed, piled her hair into a severe knot under her cap, did what she could to her face and repaired downstairs to her dinner, watched over by her motherly landlady, dying to ask questions, but knowing that there was no time to gossip. Philomena presented herself at the clinic with only minutes to spare and plunged into work. All three doctors were there, but excepting for instructions about the patients and requests for this and that, none of them, least of all Walle, had much to say to her.

The clinic finished late and they left one by one, leaving her to clear up and then take herself off for her evening meal. There was an hour or so before Doctor de Klein's evening surgery, time enough for Mevrouw de Winter to take up her position in the kitchen door while Philomena ate and ply her with questions. And Philomena, who regarded conversation of any kind as an exercise in Dutch, described the night's activities, trying out a new word here and there and trying, too, to get her tenses right, so that she had no time to herself before she made the short journey to Doctor de Klein's house. It was still a lovely evening when she had finished there, but by now she was too tired to care; she went back to her little room, carrying the cup of coffee Mevrouw de Winter had made for her, and was in bed and asleep before she could drink it.

Her days were busy, but she enjoyed them now that she felt more at ease with her work and had got over her initial shyness at speaking Dutch, and in the evenings when she was free, she took the Mini and explored the surrounding countryside, taking care never to go too near Walle's castle and refusing to admit, even to herself, that she was on occasion lonely. Everyone was kind, she told herself; she had a dozen acquaintances and had been out once or twice with Corrie. Besides, Doctor de Klein had suggested that she should join him and his family on a picnic in the near future. She wrote cheerful letters home, although no one, so far, had answered them, but her friends at Faith's wrote regularly, begging for news, so that, what with her dogged study of the Dutch language and long descriptions of her life to pen, she had little time in which to feel sorry for herself.

Saturday morning was everything that a June morning should be, still a little cool, for it was still early in the month, but the sky was blue and the sun shone. Philomena, up early, packed her overnight bag with slacks and a cotton shirt, sensible canvas shoes, and a slip of a green crêpe dress which matched her eyes, and when morning surgery was over, she rushed back to change into a cotton shirtwaister in Liberty print before getting to work on her face and hair. The result was fairly satisfactory, she decided; she would never be a beauty, but the deceptively simple hairstyle the expensive hairdresser had created for her made the most of its fine straight length, and her face, while not exactly what she would have owned, was passable. She sprayed herself with *Madame Rochas*, put on elegant sandals, picked up her bag and went downstairs, to arrive at the front door at the same moment as the doctor in the Khamsin. He wished her a cheerfully casual good morning, then got out of the car to open the door for her and take her case. She thought how elegant he looked in his sports shirt and slacks with a silk cravat tied carelessly, the elegance quite unstudied, although she guessed that it must have cost a great deal of money; possibly he was a wealthy man, she hadn't considered that seriously until that moment. Not, she hastened to remind herself, that it made the slightest difference to her whether he was rich or poor.

They talked in a friendly, desultory way as he drove

the short distance to the castle. When it came in sight Philomena asked: 'What do you call it—your castle?'

'Kasteel Tacx.'

'Oh. Did you take the name from it, or did your family give it?'

'An ancestor built it—a van der Tacx—oh, three hundred years ago or more. It took him almost a lifetime, I believe, and ever since his descendants have been adding to it, and pulling bits down and adding on wherever they fancied.'

'And have you added anything?' she wanted to know.

'I? Lord no, though I must admit that I've installed central heating.'

They had arrived at the entrance and he got out to open her door. As she stepped past him he remarked carelessly: 'You look different, though I can't think why. Probably because you're not in uniform.'

Hardly a compliment, she reflected, but at least he must have looked at her; perhaps the green dress, coupled with even more attention to the hair and face, might make him look a second time. She sighed a little as the door opened as they reached it and a tall, bony old man stood aside for them to enter.

The hall, viewed from the entrance, was even more magnificent than Philomena had remembered, the staircase rising splendidly from its further wall to the gallery above, its walls lined with paintings she had had no time to notice on her previous visit. The doctor's hand propelled her gently across the hall, not, this time, to the sitting room but to the other side, through a narrow door leading into a small, cosily furnished room with French windows open on to a vast conservatory. He didn't stop here, however, but went through another door into the garden beyond. No expense spared, Philomena told herself silently, taking in the well ordered flower beds, the smoothly raked paths and the velvet lawns stretching away to a distant shrubbery backed by trees.

There were garden chairs and tables arranged here and there and a swinging hammock. Mevrouw van der Tacx was sitting in one of the chairs, very upright, knitting, and in the hammock Tritia lay, her blonde prettiness set off by the pale blue of her sundress. She got up gracefully as they approached and came to meet them, to throw an arm round the doctor's neck and smile up at him. Philomena had the impression that if she hadn't been there the girl would have kissed him, and it afforded her a little pleasure to see that he disentangled himself gently, without taking his hand from her own arm, and went on his way to where his mother was sitting. Mevrouw van der Tacx's welcome was sincere and warm and since she included her son in the easy conversation she started, he sat down beside Philomena, apparently not noticing Tritia's attempts to entice him over to the hammock, so that presently that young lady turned a sulky shoulder and pretended to sleep.

They had coffee presently, and when his mother suggested that Philomena might like a stroll in the garden, the doctor got to his feet readily enough, and although he asked Tritia if she would like to go with them, he hardly gave her time to reply as he wandered away with Philomena beside him.

The gardens were beautiful and vast, with a formal Dutch garden at one side of the castle which led to a rose garden not yet fully in flower but still lovely enough for Philomena to exclaim over it in delight and which led, in its turn, to open parkland sloping gently down to the river.

'It's glorious!' she declared, and meant it. 'How you must love your home. Don't you wish...' she hesitated, and he finished for her:

'That I had nothing else to do but live here? Sometimes, but I love my work, Philly—it's part of my life, just as it was part of my father's.'

'It's very large.'

He smiled down at her. 'I suppose it is, although I don't notice that—besides, my mother comes to stay fairly frequently, although she lives in Friesland now, and as she is one of four sisters, I have family enough, and Tritia is living with us for the time being while one of my aunts is away—life is never dull while she is around.'

Philomena longed to make a pithy answer to this, but didn't, and because the silence became rather too lengthy as they strolled along, began to make knowledgeable remarks about roses, their growing and cultivation in general and his own magnificent collection in particular. It was rather disconcerting when he made no reply to her painstaking efforts, so that she said rather tartly: 'I expect you would like to go back now...'

He stopped abruptly and turned her round to face him, a hand under her chin so that she was forced to look at him. 'Now what on earth made you say that, Philly?'

Her candid green eyes met his blue ones. 'Well, I've been talking about roses for minutes on end and all you've done is grunt or not answer at all—I daresay you're bored.' She added quickly: 'It doesn't matter, my stepmother has tried to turn me into something interesting like Chloe or Miriam, but I'm not, you see.'

'And thank God for that,' he said gently. 'You should have a better opinion of yourself, Philly. I suspect that you grew up in the shadow of those two lovely sisters of yours and somewhere along the line you got the idea that you were plain, dull and quite uninteresting.'

He sounded very kind and she seethed inwardly, hating his pity, and seethed even more as he went on: 'You should forget all that—you're none of those things.' He waved a hand in a vague fashion. 'Do something to your hair, buy new clothes, make-up, shoes...you have beautiful eyes and when you don't screw it into that great bun, your hair is beautiful too.'

Philomena, by a superhuman effort, kept her face calm. She had been seething, now she was at boiling point, and it took all her resolution not to point out to him that she had already done all these things and he hadn't even noticed. She said sweetly: 'I must follow your good advice—I had no idea that you were so observant.'

She had no answer to his placid: 'Oh, it wasn't I who was observant—Tritia mentioned it; she's quite an expert on such things,' but he didn't seem to notice her silence, for he went on placidly: 'Would you like to go riding? I've a nice little mare which would just suit you.'

She schooled her voice to pleasant friendliness. 'I'd love that—could I ride anywhere in the park? What about the road?'

'Oh, there are several quiet lanes around here—I'll show you.'

She said a little too quickly: 'Oh, you don't have to do that, I shall enjoy pottering around on my own.' She gave him a brief smile, still swallowing rage.

'Well, I don't, so you'll have to put up with my company, Philly.' They were standing by the river, watching its clear water swirling past. 'I suppose we had better go back for lunch.'

A pleasant meal, for the doctor and his mother saw to that, making her feel at home, ignoring Tritia's sweetly barbed remarks, the doctor with good-humoured indulgence, his mother with disapproval. Philomena was heartily glad when Tritia refused to go riding with them. She had a headache, she declared, looking slyly at Walle to see what he would say. Philomena's deflated spirits were lifted a little when he merely remarked that in that case she had better go and lie down quietly until it was better.

The mare was a chestnut and not too quiet, and Walle's own mount, a great bay, was anxious for exercise. They circled the park and then took to the lanes bordering it, not talking much, letting the horses go where there was a stretch of open ground and then ambling along side by side. Philomena, in cotton shirt and slacks, her hair hanging in a thick plait down her straight little back, was, for the moment, very happy, so that the evening ahead of her, to which she hadn't been much looking forward, suddenly offered quite pleasant possibilities. She mulled them over while Walle told her about the estate and by the time they had reached the castle again she felt eager enough for them.

A needless exercise; as they made their way through the back corridors towards the hall, they were met by Mathias, the elderly manservant, with the news that Philomena was wanted on the telephone. Doctor de Klein with the news that there had been an accident; an elderly woman with severe head injuries would need to go at once to Utrecht. Philomena was to return at once and accompany the patient to hospital. 'So sorry to spoil your afternoon,' said the doctor belatedly, 'but there is no one else. You should be back by eight o'clock.' He added: 'If Doctor van der Tacx is there ask him to speak, will you?'

She handed Walle the telephone without a word. Her pleasant evening had been spoilt and there was nothing she could do about it. She waited quietly while Walle spoke to his partner and when he had finished said in her sensible way: 'I'll go and pack my bag—is there someone who could drive me back?'

'I'll drive you—and why pack a bag? You'll come back here—we'll put dinner back an hour. Come along.'

So she went as she was and driving fast, they were outside the clinic at the same time as the ambulance came to a halt before its door. The patient was on a stretcher in one of the surgeries. Walle and his partner went to look at her before she was carefully loaded in, then Walle spoke briefly to the ambulance driver, even more briefly to Philomena and got into his car again, backing it so that the ambulance could pass. Philomena, a white overall covering her slacks, was too occupied with her patient and the instructions she had been given to do more than nod absently in his direction, and it wasn't until she had handed the woman over at the hospital that she began to wonder what happened next, and the ambulance driver's tap on her shoulder settled the matter for her. She was to go back to Ommen with him and report the patient's condition to Doctor de Klein and then, presumably, await events.

Did one telephone the castle and say that one was back, she wondered, or go to one's lodgings and hope for the best? It wasn't much good guessing, so she gave

up within a short time and spent the return journey prac-
tising her Dutch on the driver, a cheerful man, only too
glad to tell her all about his wife and children and some
of the more spectacular cases he had had to deal with.
She understood quite a bit of what he was saying and
learnt a few new words as well, besides teaching him a
handful of English phrases in return. He wished her a
cheerful goodbye as he dropped her off close to the
clinic, and she turned to make her way to Doctor de
Klein's house; the clinic was closed, he would have
gone home and doubtless expected her to go there. The
church clock struck eight o'clock and she barely had
time to register that fact when she saw Walle leaning
against the bonnet of his car, watching her, and when
she exclaimed: 'Oh, I didn't expect you…' he came to
meet her with: 'What a wretched fellow you must think
me!' She could hear the laughter in his voice. 'I told the
driver to radio through when he left Utrecht.'

She beamed at him. 'Oh, how nice of you, but I have
to see Doctor de Klein.'

'I know. We'll go there now.'

It only took ten minutes or so; she gave her concise,
accurate report, was thanked warmly for her help, and
whisked back into the car.

The brief journey was taken up with the details of the
case and as they got out, Walle observed: 'Can you
manage half an hour? I told them to delay dinner, but
you've earned a drink first.'

Philomena went up to her room, to find that someone
had laid the green dress on the bed with her slippers on
the carpet; the lighted room looked welcoming, as did
the bathroom, its door invitingly open, towels draped
ready for her use. Feeling cosseted, she bathed and
changed and went downstairs with five minutes to spare,
conscious that she had made the most of herself and if
the doctor didn't notice the difference then he must be
blind.

All useless, she discovered as soon as she entered the
drawing room on the heels of Mathias, waiting in stately
patience for her in the hall. Tritia was standing in the
glow of a standard lamp between the windows, its
shadowy rose light making the most of the white
gossamer creation floating around her slim body, her
hair hanging round her lovely face, her pretty, useless
hands clasping her glass so that the pink-tinted nails
glinted and caught the eye. Philomena, taking in the fact
that Mevrouw van der Tacx was in a long dress too, had
a strong desire to turn and run, but Walle, handsome in
his black tie and dinner jacket, was already coming
towards her.

He put a kindly arm across her shoulders and
remarked in a voice just as kindly: 'What a wretched
piece of bad luck, Philly—such things happen so
seldom, and that it should have been today of all days!
Come over here and have that drink.'

He sounded like an elder brother, she thought,

sipping her sherry, and probably he regarded her in much the same light, and what was the use of fussing over her mediocre person when he didn't even look at her long enough to see that her hair was up and not in a plait? She had vowed that she would make him eat his words, but she could see now that that was nonsense; she might have given up then and there, only she looked up and caught Tritia's mocking, amused eyes on her. She smiled brilliantly at the girl and made a resolution not to give up however useless it seemed.

Dinner was as pleasant as lunch had been. Philomena, hungry after her unexpected journey, ate her way through hors d'oeuvres, sole in cream sauce, roast pheasant and a delicious sweet, a nice change from Mevrouw de Winter's wholesome, plain fare, and while she ate she listened to Walle and his mother smoothly guiding the conversation from one topic to the next, sweeping her along with them while Tritia, looking exquisite, ate with a bird's appetite and when she spoke it was in a soft little voice which would have charmed the stoniest-hearted man. And why couldn't she be like that, wondered Philomena, so that men—and by men she meant Walle, looked at her as though she were something extra special to be pandered to and spoilt. Just thinking about it made her feel gloomy, but the gloom was dispelled when, over coffee, he asked her if she would like to go riding again in the morning, and even when Tritia broke in prettily and asked if she might

go with them, she didn't mind. 'Only I simply must
have Beauty,' she declared with a pout, 'You know how
frightened I am of Bess.' She glanced at Philomena. 'I
know Philomena had Beauty today, but I'm sure she
won't mind...'

Walle gave her an indulgent smile. 'Of course she
won't—will you, Philly?'

Philomena had liked Beauty, and probably Bess
wouldn't be half such a good mount, but after all, she
was only a guest, there for a day or two, so she agreed
pleasantly and added that it was marvellous to have the
chance of a ride anyway, and earned an approving look
from the doctor for saying it.

Bess, when Philomena saw her early the next
morning, proved to be a piebald mare, with a wicked
eye, but the doctor's easy: 'She's lively, but you'll
manage her easily enough,' she took to be a compliment
so that she swung herself happily into the saddle while
Tritia, in beautifully cut jodhpurs and silk shirt which
made fun of Philomena's slacks and cotton sweater,
made a small feminine fuss about Beauty's bridle,
which she insisted on Walle attending to.

But it didn't take Philomena long to realise that the
girl didn't like riding; she sat uneasily and each time
Beauty attempted more than a walk, she was checked.
The three of them ambled along, across the park
towards the river and then turned into a narrow lane and
eventually into a water meadow beside the river. 'Bess

could do with a bit of exercise,' Philomena ventured.
'Would anyone mind…?'

It seemed that the meadow was Walle's anyway and
he raised no objection, so she touched Bess's flanks
with a heel and the mare tossed her head and broke into
a gallop. They circled the field and then, dropping to a
more sober pace, rejoined the others. The exercise had
put a glow into Philomena's cheeks and a sparkle in her
eyes, she beamed at Walle: 'That was fun! Bess is a
darling…' and had the satisfaction of hearing his: 'We
must have a race some time, Philly,' a remark which sent
Tritia into the sulks for the rest of their ride.

They all went to church later on, driving to the
village in a Daimler Sovereign with Tritia sitting in
front with the doctor, demanding prettily that he must
do this, that and the other thing for her before they
could set out; peeping at Philomena to see if she was
watching. But Philomena looked carefully the other
way, talking to Mevrouw van der Tacx, telling herself
that after all, if Tritia liked to make an exhibition of
herself that was her business, and if Walle couldn't see
through her silliness then that was his business too.

And after lunch they played croquet on the lawn at
the side of the castle—it could have been late Victorian
England, Philomena reflected, eating tea under the
trees; cucumber sandwiches and cherry cake and a maid
to carry out the tea things. She had no idea that people
still lived in that style. And after tea when she sug-

gested diffidently that it was time she returned to Ommen, Walle wouldn't hear of it.

'You'll stay for dinner,' he told her, 'and I'll drive you back later. You haven't seen Tinker and her puppies yet—she's over in the stables for a few days in peace and quiet.'

'I didn't know you had a dog—I've seen two cats...'

'Mieps and Tom. Tinker had her puppies four days ago and she'll be coming back with us in another day or so. I take her out early in the morning and again about this time when she's been fed.' He got out of his chair. 'Come with me now, if you like—Tritia doesn't like dogs, so we won't ask her.'

Tinker was a long-haired Alsatian and the puppies were adorable, and when Philomena gave her her fist to sniff she was accepted as a friend at once. They walked the dog for half an hour, the doctor covering the ground fast with his long legs and Philomena skipping along beside him, throwing sticks for Tinker while they talked and occasionally argued in a friendly fashion; they were back at the castle far too soon for Philomena.

Contrary to her expectations, dinner passed off successfully. Tritia, a vision in pale blue, was all sweetness. Her tinkling laugh made Philomena grit her teeth, but she didn't allow it to spoil her pleasure, and presently, ready to leave, she ignored her mocking smile as she wished her goodbye.

'Back to work,' said Tritia, 'but of course you are

used to that. A glimpse of life—our sort of life in this so magnificent castle—must have given you pleasure.'

Walle was talking to his mother, but he paused to intervene blandly: 'How incredibly pompous you sound, Tritia! I'm going back to work too, you know, and living in a country house is no new thing for Philomena. Her own home is a charming one in England with surroundings just as lovely as these.'

He kissed his mother, waved to Tritia and shook his head at her as he opened the car door for Philomena, but he didn't mention Tritia's rudeness during the short drive, talking about nothing much until they arrived at Mevrouw de Winter's door where he stood quietly while Philomena thanked him for her weekend.

He looked down at her, smiling a little. 'It was rather spoilt, wasn't it? We must make up for it next time.'

She had the sad thought that there was unlikely to be a next time, Tritia would see to that, and perhaps it would be as well, her suddenly surprised mind warned her; falling in love with one's rich, handsome employer was something which happened in novels, not to real girls such as she was. Returning his look, she wished him a sober goodbye, unable to detect the smallest sign that he shared her unexpected discovery. She went slowly indoors and up the cramped little stairs to her room. Cupid, she decided, was a wash-out...or perhaps he had run out of arrows.

CHAPTER SEVEN

IT WAS AS WELL for Philomena that she saw very little of Walle during the next few days. Discovering that she was in love with him had taken the wind completely out of her matter-of-fact sails, although when she thought about it, she supposed that she had been in love with him for quite a time; since the moment she had first seen him, even, and since it was hopeless to imagine that he would ever take more than a kindly interest in her, the quicker she nipped her feelings for him in the bud, the better. She was helped considerably in this praiseworthy resolution by the measles, which, neatly stamped out in Vilsteren, reared its spotty head in Dalfsen and Ommen, giving all three doctors and Philomena a good deal of extra work, and when she did find herself alone with Walle it was always in the company of a distraught young mother and small peevish children, so that any conversation they might have was brief, businesslike and strictly medical in flavour.

So it was all the more surprising, as well as making nonsense of her good resolutions to avoid him, when Walle put his head round the door as she was clearing the surgery after the last session for the day and asked her if she would like to go riding on Sunday. The next day; she thought rapidly, then looked him in the eye and lied briskly in what she hoped was a convincing manner. 'Actually,' she told him, 'I'm spending the day with Hubert,' and was disconcerted by his slow smile, although she was reassured the next instant by his:

'Ah, of course. Somewhere nice, I hope?'

'Friesland,' she improvised wildly, 'just—just to look around, you know.'

The smile came and went again. 'Of course—he has an aunt near Leeuwarden—I expect he has told you about her.' His voice was bland.

'Yes, he has,' declared Philomena, bent on bolstering up her fibs and completely at sea. 'She—she seems a very interesting person.'

Her companion's firm mouth twitched its corners, but all he said was: 'Another time, perhaps? Enjoy yourself, Philly.'

Left alone, she finished her clearing up and went back to Mevrouw de Winter's house, wondering what she would do with her free Saturday afternoon. Take the Mini for a run? Perhaps if she scouted round Leeuwarden a little just in case Walle asked questions later? But her landlady, when asked how far that city

was away, thought that it might be close on ninety kilometres, which, allowing for time to eat her dinner and
get there and back, left little time to look around the
place. Philomena reluctantly gave up the idea for a
circular tour of the surrounding countryside which
brought her back in nice time for one of Mevrouw de
Winter's substantial suppers.

Sunday, when she woke, proved to be glorious weather.
Looking from her window at eight o'clock in the morning,
she wished heartily that she had accepted the doctor's invitation. She got up and put on a sleeveless cotton dress,
piled her hair elaborately and then took it down again and
tied it back, for after all, there was no one to see, and went
down to breakfast. Her landlady had gone to church and
from there intended to visit a nephew on the other side of
the town. Philomena was to eat a good breakfast, said the
carefully written note on the mantelpiece, and make
herself coffee, and if she went out, she was to be sure and
see that the cat was in and the back door locked.

Philomena ate her meal leisurely, washed up, tidied
the table and sat down to decide what to do with her day.
Leeuwarden seemed the logical answer—it was a pity
that Hubert wasn't there to take her; she hadn't liked
telling lies to Walle. As if in answer to her wish there
was a resounding thump on the front door knocker.
'That's him,' she told herself aloud, and was conscious
of reluctance to spend a whole day with him after all,
despite the fact that it would wipe out all her fibbing.

She went to the door, her face expressing a mixture of annoyance and relief, both of which were wiped away at the sight of Walle outside.

His good morning was placid although his eyes held a pronounced twinkle, but she didn't notice that as she mumbled an uncertain good morning back at him.

'Not gone yet?' he asked chattily.

'No—no…' She paused because for the life of her she couldn't think of anything to say. At length: 'A case?' she sounded almost hopeful.

'No, Philly. Neither of us is on call.' He added gently: 'What a shocking little liar you are.'

She went pink. 'Me? Oh!'

'Oh, indeed. You should do your homework before you start making up stories about going out for the day. Hubert is on duty this weekend, and he certainly has no aunts in Friesland. Now I have got a grandfather in Schouwen Duiveland, a genuine relation with whom I intend having lunch. I thought you might like to come along too.'

She drew a slow breath. 'Well…' she paused, frowning. 'I told you a lot of—of lies. I'm sorry. It's very kind of you to ask me, but I can't come, thank you all the same.'

'Can't or won't?' He looked up at the blue sky; it really was a splendid day. 'I expect I should have done exactly the same thing if I had been you,' he observed in a nice impersonal voice. 'Besides, I told Grandfather that I should be bringing you.'

Philomena gaped at him. 'But you didn't ask…how could you know?…and how very high-handed,' she finished haughtily. She spoilt it by adding: 'Isn't there anything else you'd rather do?'

He looked as though he was going to laugh. 'Not a thing. Mother has gone visiting and Tritia is fully occupied with one of her youthful hangers-on.'

So that's why I've been asked, thought Philomena sadly, he's at a loose end. She looked up and caught his eye and he shook his head at her.

'Your thoughts are clear on your face, Philly, and they're all wrong. Where's Mevrouw de Winter? Shall we let her know?'

'She's at church and she's going to have coffee with a nephew; if I go out I'm to let the cat in and lock the back door—and I must do my hair…'

'It looks quite all right as it is, leave it alone. I'll write a note for Mevrouw de Winter while you see to the cat.'

He went past her into the hall and sat down at the kitchen table, where he got out a notebook and pen and began to scrawl rapidly. By the time Philomena had settled the cat, fetched her handbag and found the front door key, he was standing waiting for her. Five minutes later they were out of the little town, heading south.

'It's about a hundred and seventy miles,' he explained as they took the road to Deventer. 'We'll keep to the motorway for a good deal of the way; we can join it at Appeldoorn, go on to Utrecht and Rotterdam and turn off for Willemstad. Coming back we'll take the country roads as much as we can, that way you'll see something of Holland.'

Philomena, rather vague as to where they were going, said how nice and settled back to enjoy the pleasure of the moment. It struck her forcibly that although she had been in his car on several occasions, the journeys had been short and usually taken in haste. Now she had the chance to savour the luxury of the car's interior. She sighed with pleasure. The road ran before them, tree lined and as yet, fairly empty of traffic, it was almost thirty miles before they would reach the motorway, the weather was perfect, and the whole long day stretched before her. She buried Tritia deep in the back of her mind and prepared to enjoy herself.

Something in which Walle was prepared to share; they talked and laughed together as the miles flew past and presently, through Amersfoort, and with Utrecht already on the horizon, they stopped for coffee at a roadside café before he took the car through the heart of the city to join the motorway on its other side. 'Sunday,' he explained, 'and not much traffic, although I wouldn't recommend it to anyone who doesn't know Utrecht blindfold.' They seemed to be in the outskirts of Rotterdam in no time at all and Philomena lost all sense of direction as Walle drove his way round and south once more to Barendrecht. The roads were busy by now, but he didn't seem to mind, only drove steadily

and very fast, never hesitating. They didn't go into
Willemstad but kept on the motorway still, leaving the
pretty little town with its windmill and harbour to fade
into the distance. They were almost there, Walle told
her, pointing out that they were among the islands of
Zeeland now, with water all round them, alive with
sailing boats and Zierikzee signposted straight ahead.
'Only we're not going as far as that,' he went on, 'we
turn off here.'

The village they were going through was common-
place enough and Philomena felt vague disappoint-
ment—she had expected something picturesque and
old and away from the main road. But she wasn't disappointed after all. The country road they had turned
into was narrow and brick-built, running between flat
fields full of cows. The motorway seemed very far
away, and after a few minutes' driving, Walle turned off
this road too, into a still narrower one which dived
suddenly between tall trees.

'Here we are,' he said, and slowed to round the gentle
curve in the road.

The village of Schuttebeurs was small, nothing
indeed, but the country road shrouded by trees and lined
by a handful of pleasant villas, a nice old country house
which had been skilfully modernised into an hotel and
one or two large houses, standing well back from the
road as though, because of their size and age, they had
no intention of mixing with their more modern neigh-

bours. It was before one of these that he stopped the car; a tall, flat-fronted mansion, almost concealed by trees and shrubs and enclosed by a high iron railing. There was nothing remarkable about it, but it looked solid and peaceful, its high wide windows sparkling in the sunshine, the formal flower beds on either side of the short drive filled with flowers. Philomena, skipping out as Walle opened the door for her, rotated slowly, admiring it all until he took her arm and marched her up to the door, a solid affair with a heavy brass knocker and an old-fashioned bell-pull beside it.

But there was no need to use either of these. The door was opened as they reached it, by a tall angular woman of uncertain age, dressed severely in black, whose equally severe features broke into a smile as Walle flung an arm round her shoulders and kissed her cheek.

'Annie, Philly, she has been with my grandfather for most of her life—you'll have to try out your Dutch; she speaks no English.'

Philomena put out a hand and spoke up gravely, getting a bit muddled, but Annie didn't seem to mind, for she smiled and shook the hand repeatedly and talked back at Philomena before ushering them into the hall.

It was long and narrow and very high-ceilinged, with an ornate plastered ceiling and red damask walls, and they went past the staircase, at right angles to it, in order to reach the double doors at its end. Annie threw them open with something of a flourish, disclosing a

large square room with big windows overlooking the
grounds at the back of the house and furnished with a
great deal of mahogany and red leather. A particularly
large armchair was drawn up to one of the windows and
in it was seated an old man who looked round as they
went in and then stood up. He was almost as tall as his
grandson, with a splendid head crowned with white
hair, and even in old age, his good looks were still
striking. He greeted the doctor with evident pleasure
and then took leisurely stock of Philomena—a look she
bore with equanimity, looking back at him with candid
eyes.

'H'm—so this is Philomena.' He had a deep voice
and his English was slow and deliberate. His blue eyes,
as blue as his grandson's, raked her from head to foot.
'No looks, lovely eyes, pretty figure…going to marry
her, Walle?'

'Yes,' said Walle

Philomena took her green gaze from the old gentleman's face and looked at the doctor, who was standing
there smiling at her as though he hadn't uttered a single
preposterous word. She felt the colour leaving her face
and then rush back into it while her heart, instead of con-
tinuing its unobtrusive beating under her ribs, had jumped
into her throat, so that speaking, let alone drawing a
breath, was an impossibility. And that was a good thing
in a way, because all the elder of the two gentlemen,
looking at her so fixedly, said was: 'A glass of sherry

before lunch, don't you think? Come and sit beside me, my dear, and tell me what you think of Holland, though I daresay you have seen little enough of it.'

Philomena had found her voice. She replied with a calmness which surprised her: 'Well, I haven't been here very long, but what I've seen I like...'

'We work her too hard.' Walle had poured the sherry and was handing it round. 'Although,' he added wickedly, 'she has every hope of going to Friesland— Hubert Stanversen fancies her.'

She choked. 'That's nonsense and you know it, and you have no right...'

He interrupted her smoothly. 'Well, no, perhaps not just yet—I'm rather in the position of a child who having marked down the nicest cake on the plate for his own, hopes desperately that no one else will want it.' He smiled at her, a slow, sweet smile which made her gulp. 'Probably it makes him over-possessive towards it.'

Philomena had never been likened to a piece of cake; she supposed it was a compliment. She made herself look away from Walle because if she didn't she was in grave danger of believing every word that he said, and remarked sedately: 'The view from this room is delightful. Are you a keen gardener, Mijnheer van der Tacx?'

She was bitterly disappointed when both gentlemen plunged readily enough into a horticultural discussion which lasted until Annie arrived to tell them that lunch was on the table.

Walle's grandfather might have been old, but he had lost none of his zest for living. The meal was elaborate and elegantly served, with a young girl waiting on them, and the master of the house ate with the appetite and pleasure of a young man while he carried on a conversation which ranged from reminiscences of his youth to the discovery of oil in the North Sea, interlarded with a good many asides concerning various members of the family, and he broke off in the middle of one of such tales to ask suddenly of Philomena: 'Well, my dear, do you suppose you are going to like us? We are a good-tempered lot on the whole, although we have nasty tempers when we are crossed, but I daresay you will learn quickly enough how to turn Walle round your thumb.'

She looked at him helplessly, conscious that Walle was laughing softly. She would have liked to have pointed out that she hadn't been asked to join the family anyway; that his grandson was enjoying a joke; that he had no intention of marrying her, but she liked the old man and she wasn't going to upset him. She said calmly: 'Very probably. You said that you had a nephew in America. Does he come to Holland to see you?'

Her red herring was successful, for her host launched himself into a series of tales about his nephew, and presently they got up from the table and went back into the study to drink their coffee. Mijnheer van der Tacx dozed off almost immediately and Philomena, refusing to meet Walle's eye, sat staring into her cup with painful intensity until he said quietly: 'You didn't believe me, did you?'

'No.'

'Why not?' He leaned over and took her cup away and then sat back, the picture of contented ease.

She thought carefully before she answered him. 'A great many reasons.'

'One will do.'

'I should have thought that they were obvious enough.'

He looked amused. 'Playing for time, Philly?'

She answered indignantly: 'No, I'm not! You heard your grandfather—no looks, he said, and he's quite right. And for another thing you don't know me, and then there's Tritia…'

'Ah—the crux of the matter. And what has she got to do with us?'

Philomena pinkened, but now she had got started it seemed silly not to get the wretched matter cleared up. 'I presume that you're going to marry her…'

She got no further, because his shout of laughter stopped her although his grandfather's eyes remained closed. 'And what in heaven's name makes you think that?' he wanted to know.

Philomena considered. If she said: 'Because Tritia doesn't like me,' he might just stare, not understanding, although another woman would know what she meant at once. She could of course say because the girl loved him, but if he hadn't already realised that, there was a danger that it might kindle his interest... She was saved from saying anything at all by old Mijnheer van der Tacx, who woke at that moment enquiring in an innocent voice if there was any more coffee in the pot and would they care to take a stroll in the garden.

She followed Walle, willy-nilly, out into the bright sunshine and listened while he pointed out various flowers and shrubs, told her a little of the history of the house, and enlarged upon various aspects of his grand-father's life, and all the while she was waiting for him to say something else, only he didn't. She could have dreamed it all. She damped down a wild desire to ask him if he had indeed said that he was going to marry her, and made suitable replies to his gentle conversation, and felt nothing but relief when at length he suggested that they might go indoors again.

'Grandfather will have finished his nap by now,' he said easily, 'and be wanting a cup of tea. I thought we might leave after that.'

Philomena wasn't sure what she had expected; it looked as though he would drive her straight back to Ommen in time for her supper with Mevrouw de Winter. Perhaps he was impatient with her for not replying to his joke in kind, perhaps, and this was indeed a lowering thought, he had guessed that she had almost believed him, although she had denied that. He

would be feeling embarrassed and anxious to be rid of
her company so that they could meet again the follow-
ing day on a professional footing without any awk-
wardness. She accompanied him back into the study,
making conversation a little too brightly, and found
their host awake and indeed demanding his tea, a brief,
chatty interlude; she couldn't help but see that Walle
showed no sign of embarrassment and although they left
shortly afterwards, he seemed quite unhurried. It wasn't
until they were well away from the village that he
observed: 'I have a surprise for you, Philly.'

Nothing, she decided silently, would ever surprise
her again. Aloud she said pleasantly: 'Oh? What is it?'

'An old friend of mine—we were at medical school
together, Christian van Duyl—he and his wife have
invited us for dinner. They live near a small town called
Druten, some miles this side of Nijmegen. She's an
English girl, Eliza—they've been married three years
or so. I think you might like her.'

'It sounds delightful, but isn't Nijmegen rather a
long way?'

'Lord, no. We go through Breda and Tilburg—it's on
the way back, about a hundred and thirty miles altogether and sixty odd miles from Ommen.'

They were on the road to Bergen-op-Zoom now and
travelling fast. Philomena, torn between delight at the
prospect of the evening in Walle's company and a
feeling of deep annoyance at his earlier remarks,

decided that being annoyed was a waste of time and settled back to listen to his gentle flow of talk; information about the towns they travelled through, the quiet land around them and some of its history. Indeed, by the time they had neared their journey's end, she had quite forgotten to be annoyed and when she allowed herself to think about it briefly, she was inclined to think that she had exaggerated her feelings about the matter. Any other girl would have taken his joking in good part and she had been a fool not to do the same.

The friend was evidently as well endowed with the world's goods as Walle; the house which came into view as they rounded the curve of the drive was large and impressive, although it wasn't as old as the castle.

They were met at the door by an elderly man whom Walle addressed as Hub and who led them indoors into a vast hall, grandly furnished, and then melted into the background as two people came through a door towards them. A striking couple; the man tall and dark and as big as Walle, the girl small and very pretty, with golden hair swept into a coil on top of her head. Philomena, swept away on the warmth of their greeting, found herself in a smallish room, very elegantly furnished but cosy nonetheless, where she was sat down in a chintz-covered chair and given a glass of sherry.

'I'll take you upstairs presently,' promised Eliza. 'Dinner isn't until eight o'clock. Tell me, how do you like Holland?'

'What I've seen I like very much…'

'Oh, good—it grows on you. Ommen's a dear little place, isn't it? What do you think of Walle's castle?'

Philomena said cautiously: 'It's rather breathtaking.' She smiled at the fairylike creature beside her. 'But this house is breathtaking too.'

'That's what I thought the first time I saw it, but now it's home.' Eliza looked across to where her husband stood talking to Walle. 'Mind you,' she added, 'home would be anywhere where Christian and baby Chris are.'

'I didn't know you had a baby. How old is he?'

The two of them became engrossed until Christian reminded them that dinner was only ten minutes away and wouldn't Philomena like to tidy herself first?

So the two girls went upstairs, visiting the nursery on the way, so that the ten minutes became twenty before they joined the men again.

'We had to peep in on baby,' explained Eliza. 'Walle, you must see him before you go—he's grown.' Her tone implied that the infant had done something miraculous and her husband smiled down at her with loving amusement.

'They do, you know, my love. Hub has been to the door twice and coughed—I fancy we're keeping dinner waiting.'

The meal was a merry one and the food delicious; moreover they drank champagne with it so that Philomena, already feeling at home with her host and hostess, began to enjoy herself. She was sampling a delicate sorbet when Eliza asked: 'What are we celebrating? I mean, the champagne? Is it someone's birthday?'

'No, my love, and I think that perhaps celebrating is rather a premature gesture. Shall I say that we're celebrating a hopeful wish?'

Eliza might be small and helpless to look at, but she was a forthright girl. 'Oh, you mean Walle and Philomena.' She beamed at Philomena, who had gone a bright, becoming pink. 'Sorry if I've put my foot in it. I quite thought from looking at you both…'

Philomena said composedly: 'It's quite all right.'

She was interrupted ruthlessly by Walle. 'The poor girl doesn't know if she's coming or going—Grandfather jumped the gun this morning and since I—er—hadn't mentioned the matter, she feels in rather a muddle. Isn't that so, Philly?'

'Yes,' said Philomena, and didn't look at him.

Christian took the champagne from its silver bucket and refilled their glasses. 'There is nothing like champagne to clear up a muddle,' he observed cheerfully. 'What do you think of this one, Walle?'

'Dom Perignon 1970,' said Walle promptly. 'I've some myself, though I quite like a Krug.' The two men drifted easily into a discussion about wines and Philomena, her colour normal once more, went on with her dinner, answering Eliza's happy chatter while she firmly ignored the bewildered thoughts racing around inside her head.

The conversation for the rest of the evening was exemplary. It wasn't until they were on the point of leaving that Eliza said happily: 'Of course, we shall see you again, Philomena—isn't it nice that Christian and Walle are such old friends? We'll be able to visit each other, and think how splendid it will be for the children...'

Philomena took care not to look at the men. Probably, she thought crossly, Walle would be holding back a laugh. She agreed in a rather faint voice because she could really think of nothing else to say and got into the car in a silence which wasn't broken for quite a few minutes, and then it was Walle who spoke.

'Poor Philly, everything has conspired to puzzle you—you don't know what to believe, do you?' He went on in a matter-of-fact voice: 'Of course, I could propose to you here and now, but I don't intend to; it's neither the time nor the place—we'll have to wait for a suitable moment.'

He didn't wait for her to reply, which was just as well, as she had none ready. 'Did you enjoy your day? I did—Grandfather may be an old man, but he's still very with it, although since my father died he has become much more subdued.'

'When did your father die?' She seized on the chance to start a normal conversation, although her voice wobbled annoyingly.

'A year ago; he wasn't old—sixty-seven—but he

went out on a bitter cold night and caught a chill which became pneumonia—it was well advanced by the time he was seen, he hadn't a chance.'

'I'm sorry.'

'He would have liked you, Philly, and I think that you would have liked him. A pity he couldn't have seen us married.'

Philomena caught her breath. And what did she say to that? she wondered. Chloe or Miriam would have known exactly how to handle the situation; she wished fervently that she had some of their self-assurance. But she hadn't. She asked in a small voice: 'Are you like him?'

'So I'm told, and I'm glad.' They were tearing through the Veluwe now although there was little to see save the wooded heath on either side of the road picked up by the headlights, and presently Walle turned off on to the Loenen road on to a minor road which led them eventually to Deventer. They were more than halfway home and he, Philomena realised, had no intention of talking seriously. He entertained her with titbits of information about the villages and towns they went through, talked a good deal about hospital life in Holland, enquired after her own family and asked how she liked living at Mevrouw de Winter's house.

'Very nice, thank you,' said Philomena sedately, 'and I have endless opportunities to speak Dutch.'

'Good, the quicker you learn it the better. There's a pretty busy clinic tomorrow, I believe.'

They talked of this and that for the rest of the journey. The roads were emptier now, for it was late, indeed the church clock at Ommen was striking half past twelve as Walle stopped before the little house. He got out and opened Philomena's door and when she started to wish him goodnight, stopped her with an airy, 'Oh, I'm coming in for a cup of coffee. Mevrouw de Winter will have one ready for us.'

And he was right. Her landlady, cosily dressing-gowned, was waiting for them in the kitchen with the best cups and saucers on a tray and the coffee pot simmering on a gas ring. She would have carried the tray through to the front parlour, only the doctor wouldn't allow that, declaring that he liked kitchens and Mevrouw de Winter's in particular, and went on to ask after her family with the genuine interest of a long-standing friend. He didn't hurry. It was striking one o'clock when he got to his feet and bade Mevrouw de Winter a courteous goodnight. 'Philomena will see me out, won't you, Philly?' he added.

The little hall seemed over-full with them both standing in it. Philomena made herself as small as possible against the wall and wished him goodnight. Even in her own ears, her voice sounded rather breathless.

She was plucked from the wall as though she had been a handful of feathers. The doctor didn't say a word, only kissed her in such a manner that she was kept awake half the night remembering it.

CHAPTER EIGHT

PHILOMENA NEED NOT have missed her sleep. Walle, when she met him at the clinic in the morning, was brisk and impersonal, certainly not the same man who had kissed her the previous evening. He dealt with his patients with his usual calm patience but wasted no time when he had finished—indeed, she came out of one of the surgeries to get something for Doctor de Klein to see his massive back going through the door. It wasn't until the very last patient had gone that Doctor Stanversen casually mentioned that Doctor van der Tacx wouldn't be in for a few days. He didn't give a reason and Philomena didn't like to ask.

The week crawled by, despite the fact that they were busier than usual. Philomena filled her free time with short trips to neighbouring towns and the writing of lengthy letters to her friends at Faith's—she wrote home too, despite the fact that she would get no reply. Her stepmother had telephoned, not so much to discover how she fared as to tell her that they would be going away for a week or so. 'Scotland,' she had said, 'though exactly where I'm not sure—some remote lodge, I believe. It's not the fashionable time to go, but the MacPhersons have invited us and I believe their lodge is rather super. They have that nice boy of theirs staying, too—a little older than Chloe.' She had forgotten to ask Philomena if she were happy in Ommen, although she did suggest that she stayed there for as long as she liked.

Philomena had put down the receiver feeling unwanted. She had told herself briskly that she was being silly; her stepmother was fond of her in her own way, it was just that Philomena had never quite fitted in with their way of life. All the same she felt a lot better when Hubert telephoned to ask her if she would spend Saturday afternoon with him; a drive to Kampen, he suggested, and tea somewhere on the way back. He would have to be back in Utrecht for dinner with friends, he was sure she would understand...

She wasn't sure what she was supposed to understand, it was only when they were on their way that she discovered his reason for wishing to get back in good time. There was a girl, he confided, apparently possessing all the attributes of a beauty queen as well as an intelligence seldom seen in women, and this topped off with a disposition which sounded too good to be true. Philomena listened patiently to his eulogy, made suitable comments when she could get a word in edgeways and offered the encouragement he undoubtedly hoped she would give him. By the time they were half way to Kampen she was heartily sick of the girl, but she was too kind to allow her impatience to show; she lent a sympathetic ear, murmured from time to time and allowed her thoughts to stray.

They were within sight of Kampen and about to cross the river Ijssel when they were held up for a moment on the bridge. There was a great deal of traffic and Philomena watched it idly. The Khamsin with Walle at the wheel and Tritia beside him passed them, going in the opposite direction. Tritia was laughing and talking, Walle was looking ahead of him, but as he drew level he glanced sideways to encounter Philomena's fiery eye. There was no chance to see his expression. Hubert edged the car forward and at the same time the Khamsin had gone, leaving only the echo of a subdued roar, and Philomena, swallowing the unpleasant medley of feelings churning around inside her, began a feverish series of questions about Kampen, its houses, the charm of the buildings lining the water and the surrounding country, all tumbling out one after the other so that Hubert, rather puzzled because she had asked the same questions during their previous visit, and still mentally with the paragon he was going to meet that evening, had no chance to answer any of them.

She was so unlike her usual serene self for the rest

of the afternoon that Hubert gave her a puzzled look from time to time and even asked her if she felt all right, to which she replied with quite unnatural vivacity that she had never felt better. They explored the town for an hour or so before having tea and cakes at De Stadsherberg, and on the return journey Philomena abandoned her lively chatter and encouraged Hubert to talk about his paragon, something he was by no means loath to do; it kept him fully occupied for the whole trip and enabled her to think her own not very happy thoughts while she said 'Yes' and 'No' and 'How fascinating' whenever he paused for breath. But once indoors with Mevrouw de Winter she was forced to describe her outing down to the last crumb of cake, an exercise which, undertaken in her still sparse Dutch, took all her concentration. She longed to go to her room and brood over Walle, but that would have hurt her landlady's feelings, so she sat through supper, still talking, and then spent another hour after they had washed up together, looking at a family photo album Mevrouw de Winter produced as a special treat.

When Philomena eventually got to bed she was so befuddled by her efforts to make herself understood in the Dutch language that she fell asleep at once, quite worn out.

She was awakened by the rattle of pebbles against her open window. It was light and the sun was up, but it was barely six o'clock. She got out of bed, wild ideas of emergencies, accidents, and premature babies crowding her sleepy head. But it was none of these; it was Walle on his great horse, leading Beauty.

'Good morning, Philly, I thought we might ride together.' He grinned up at her. 'I'll give you five minutes to put on something sensible!'

Philomena blushed and withdrew as much of her as possible without disappearing from the window altogether. 'I was asleep,' she hissed severely.

'Well, I should hope so. Now hurry up, there's a good girl. We'll telephone Mevrouw de Winter later.'

Philomena had withdrawn her head, now she popped it out again. 'Why?'

'Well, she'll wonder where you are, goose.'

'But won't I be back for breakfast?'

'No.' He glanced at his watch. 'Four minutes, Philly.'

It took just a little longer; after all, she had to wash her face and tie back her hair after she had flung on slacks and a shirt. She had never looked plainer than she did now, the early sun highlighting her nondescript features, free of make-up, and yet the look on the doctor's face was all tenderness. He got off his horse while she mounted Beauty, and then swung himself up again. 'Shall we go along by the river?' he asked. 'There's a path of sorts and there's no hurry.'

The dew was still on the grass and a rabbit or two scuttled away as they left the road and took to the bridle path. The sun was well up now, but it was still quiet except for the birds and some late lambs bleating and the lazy clip-clop of their horses' hooves. Philomena, happy now, not caring about the puzzling past or the problematical future, nudged Beauty to a gentle trot and presently when the path opened out into a water meadow asked: 'Could we gallop, just for a few minutes?' And then: 'I suppose this is your land too?'

The doctor sounded almost apologetic. 'Well, yes, it is, although I rent it out, but the farmer won't object. He'll be moving his cows in later on, but for the moment it can be ours.'

The exercise brought the pink to Philomena's cheeks and loosed her hair from its ribbon. She sighed gustily with content, slowed her mount to a sedate walk and allowed her to pick her way along the bridle path once more. They were close to the water now and Philomena called suddenly: 'Look, fish!' and dismounted to get a better look.

Walle took the reins from her and led the two horses to a nearby tree stump where he made them fast and then joined her. 'Pike,' he informed her. 'Do you fish?'

She turned to look at him. 'Me? No,' she shuddered. 'They're so slippery, and I couldn't bear to take the hook out of them...'

Walle was standing very close to her, now he turned her round to face him and caught her close. 'But you eat them out of newspaper, my darling—all mixed up with tears, too.'

She stared up at him, her mouth a little open. 'Oh, you can't mean that,' she whispered.

'Of course I mean it—I shared your supper, remember?'

'Not my supper—you called me your darling.'

'You are my darling. And don't pretend that you're surprised—you heard me tell Grandfather that I was going to marry you, and I did tell you that we would have to wait for a suitable time and place, did I not? And that is now, my dearest Philly, with not a soul in sight and all day before us. I want you for my wife and I want you to say yes.' His eyes searched hers. 'I think that you love me too and I believe we can be very happy together.'

'Oh, we can, and I do love you, Walle, only I thought it was Tritia you wanted, not me—she's so very pretty and I'm not, you see.' She hesitated. 'And another thing, I'm not used to living in a castle—I'm not sure that I would suit…'

His eyes danced with laughter. 'My darling, you will be marrying me, not the castle, and I think you will suit very well. Marry me, Philly.'

She hadn't taken her eyes from his face and he was smiling down at her with gentle urgency.

'All right,' said Philly, 'I will.' She added: 'Although I'm not at all sure that it will work.'

He didn't answer at once, only held her even tighter and bent to kiss her. Presently he asked softly: 'Still not sure, Philly?'

She stared up at him. 'Well, I…you see, it's… Walle, the first time we met it was only for a minute or two, you couldn't have fallen in love with me then, and the second time and the third time you helped me, and each time I was a bit low you seemed to be there. You're not just sorry for me? Someone or other said that pity was akin to love…'

He was looking at her with no expression on his face at all and she wasn't sure if he was angry; all the same she went on: 'And now I'm working for you and you don't really *see* me, if you know what I mean.' She drew a resolute breath. 'Besides, I'm a plain girl and quite without attraction.'

He kissed her again, rather more thoroughly. 'Dear little Philly, now you will listen to me; I have never heard such a lot of nonsense in all my life! To begin with, how do you know if I fell in love with you on sight? It has happened, you know, and why should I spend hours waiting for you in that draughty entrance hall at Faith's, on the chance of you going that way? You say that I don't see you. Does it surprise you to know that I've watched your change in hairstyles, your careful make-up, your pretty clothes? I've enjoyed them all, but it would have made no difference if you had done none of these things.'

She stirred against him. 'Well, I thought you hadn't noticed a thing! You said that your partner wanted a sensible girl with no nonsense and no prospect of getting married, so you couldn't have cared a cent for me...'

The doctor kissed the top of her head with evident pleasure. 'Wrong, my darling girl. How else was I to get you—you were so sure that you were all these things, weren't you? And you're not, you know.'

She drew back to look up at him. 'But I am—Chloe and Miriam have told me, and they should know, they're so pretty and popular.'

'And quite empty, my darling. Now you, you're full of surprises—you're kind and sweet and suddenly cross in the most enchanting way, so no more nonsense. You happen to be exactly what I want.'

She slid her arms round his neck and kissed him. 'That sounds awfully nice.' She added doubtfully: 'I haven't been working here long. What do I do? Give a month's notice and go back home, or wait until you can find someone else...?'

'No waiting, Philly, there's no need of that. We'll start looking for another nurse right away. We can be married where you like. It takes a little while to arrange things here; we could have a special licence in England—perhaps you would rather be married from your home?'

'I hadn't thought about it, at least, sometimes—before I met you—I used to think that I'd like to go somewhere very quiet and just get married with no one there.'

'We'll do exactly as you wish, Philly, only let us

marry soon; I've wasted so many years before I met you.'

'There are still plenty of years left, Walle,' said Philomena softly. 'I can't quite believe it.' She slipped from his arms and smiled up at him. 'I can't imagine living in your castle.'

He took her arm and led her to where two patient horses were standing. 'You'll love it. We'll go there now and have breakfast and tell my mother.'

Philomena was on the mare, fiddling with the reins, not looking at him. 'Will she be surprised?'

'I imagine not. I haven't told her that I intended to marry you, but she will know, I think.' He leaned across and took her hand. 'She will be very happy, Philly, she's fond of you already.'

'And Tritia? I don't think she likes me—and your aunt, the one who has been away?'

'Perhaps Tritia is envious of you—she leads an aimless existence and she's almost always bored, but she's too lazy to do anything about it. But why worry about her, my darling? She will be leaving very shortly; my aunt came back last night—you will see her today, but I don't suppose she will stay long. She has a house in den Haag and much prefers living there, or so she says.'

They were allowing the horses to amble along, the sun warm on their backs now, the castle's roof visible among the trees ahead of them. Philomena reined in Beauty suddenly. 'I can't!' she declared. 'I simply can't—I haven't even brushed my hair properly and I only washed my face...'

'It looks nice,' observed the doctor, and meant it, 'but if it bothers you I'm sure whatever it is you want can be provided.'

He spoke with easy assurance, but Philomena thought privately that it would be most unlikely that the castle would yield the particular brand of cosmetics she had so extravagantly purchased for herself before she left London. But she was wrong; the bathroom to which she was led held a selection of creams and powders and lotions, as well as brushes and combs and toothbrushes. She took her time with them and was well satisfied with the result when at length she went downstairs. And judging by the doctor's behaviour, he was well satisfied too. Indeed, her hair was sadly disarranged and as her protests were half-hearted, it looked quite deplorable. She shook it out and re-tied it, then at his suggestion followed him to the study, a room she had not yet entered.

It was a large room, lined with bookshelves, and with a massive desk before its one big window. It was comfortably furnished with easy chairs and reading tables and there was a great cupboard along one of its walls. The doctor unlocked this, pressed a small knob within and revealed a wall safe, which he opened.

Philomena, at his elbow, peered in. 'What's in there?'

'Something for you, Philly.' He took out a small velvet-

covered box and opened it to show her a ring; five large
rubies bordered by diamonds, set in heavy gold. 'It's old;
it was my great-grandmother's and my grandmother left
it to me, to be given to my bride when I married.'

'Walle, I've never had anything so magnificent—
it's beautiful!'

He had taken her hand and was putting the ring on
to her finger; it fitted too and he observed: 'I have been
a little worried that your finger would be too small—
you have little hands; pretty ones too.' He kissed them
in turn and then for good measure kissed her mouth.

There was no one in the breakfast room when they
sat down at the table, but Mevrouw van der Tacx came
in shortly after, wished them good morning, allowed her
son to serve her with her breakfast from the sideboard
and then observed happily: 'You're wearing the ring,
my dear. I'm to congratulate you, Walle, am I not, and
wish you both happiness.' She got up and kissed
Philomena warmly. 'I couldn't wish for a nicer
daughter,' she declared. 'Walle's a lucky man. When are
you going to get married?'

'Just as soon as it can be arranged,' her son told her,
so that she immediately fell to making plans, some of
them very light-hearted, and there was a good deal of
laughter, interrupted by the entry of Mevrouw van Niep.

The doctor's aunt was actually no relation but the
widow of his mother's brother. She was a tall, thin lady,
with a long solemn face, light blue eyes and rigorously

coiffed hair. Her dress was fashionable but sombre and she had never, for one moment of her life, forgotten that she was from *adel*, even though she had a good deal less money than she could have wished.

She uttered a general good morning as she entered and then waited, her head on one side, looking at Philomena, who looked back, slightly unnerved by the scrutiny.

'This is Philomena Parsons, Tante Lia,' introduced the doctor. 'We are to be married in the near future.'

Philomena fancied that the pale eyes became icy, although Mevrouw van Niep smiled at her. 'How delightful—I had already heard of you, of course. Tritia has told me a great deal about you.' She was seated now, sipping her coffee and nibbling toast. 'A nurse, are you not?'

'That's right,' said Philomena cheerfully. 'I've been here several weeks now—in Ommen, you know.' She wasn't sure that she liked the lady, but she was so happy that she was disposed to like everyone, even Tritia. She heard that young lady's aunt remark now that the dear girl would be arriving after lunch. 'She has been visiting,' she explained, 'distant connections of mine, Baron Termenacht and his wife.' She paused to see what effect this information had upon Philomena, who, not having studied the Dutch *adel*, remained unimpressed. It was left for the doctor to say placidly: 'I drove her there yesterday, Philly. Two of the dullest people I have ever met.'

His aunt gave him a shocked glance and his mother laughed softly. 'Oh, I must agree. I can't think why you keep up your acquaintance with them, Lia.' Her sister-in-law gave her an indignant look and she went on placatingly: 'Oh, they have a title, I know, but who cares about that? After all, our own name is a good deal older and far more noble; I'm always thankful that our ancestors refused to be ennobled.' She smiled at Philomena. 'I'm sure you would much rather be Mevrouw than Baronne or Jonkvrouw, wouldn't you, my dear?'

'Oh, rather,' agreed Philomena happily, and fell to brooding on the delights of being called Mevrouw van der Tacx. She said dreamily: 'I like your name,' and Walle laughed and said that if she had finished her breakfast, he proposed to show her round the castle, an excursion which took up a good part of the morning and afforded them both a great deal of pleasure.

The four of them had lunch together later, and leaving the two older ladies to sit in the drawing room, Walle took Philomena into the gardens where after an exhaustive tour, they ended up playing croquet. Philomena was addressing her ball in a very professional manner when she was completely put off her stroke by the arrival of Tritia. She must try and like the girl, she reminded herself, watching her trip across the lawn towards them and all at once aware that she was still wearing the very ordinary slacks and shirt she had put on in such a hurry that morning; she couldn't attempt to match Tritia's cool perfection, nothing she had on could come near to the linen two-piece and the exquisite high-heeled sandals. She glanced down at her own everyday person and saw her ring—that was something Tritia hadn't got. Philomena allowed her hand to rest on her mallet so that the rubies caught fire in the sun.

Tritia saw it; she paused for a second, then hurried on to cast herself in Walle's arms and kiss him—an action which he suffered with equanimity but, Philomena was glad to see, a total absence of interest. Nor did he hesitate to announce their engagement, and Philomena, submitting to Tritia's congratulatory kiss, had to admit that the girl was hiding her surprise and probably chagrin very well. The croquet was abandoned after that and they went back into the castle and presently had tea, sitting in the sunshine of the verandah leading from the drawing room. And because dinner that evening was to be some sort of a celebration, Walle took Philomena back to Mevrouw de Winter's house and waited for her while she changed into a dress more suitable to the occasion and piled her hair carefully, achieving such good results that he declared that she was the prettiest girl he had ever set eyes on, a totally satisfactory and untrue remark which pleased her mightily.

They had champagne that evening and a delicious succession of dishes which Philomena ate without really noticing what they were; she would have been content with bread and cheese, just as long as Walle was there.

And after dinner Walle carried her off to his study to discuss what was to be done next. He would have liked her to have left the clinic then and there, but that wasn't possible, they both agreed about that, but he was firmly insistent that she should leave Mevrouw de Winter's and live in the castle.

'Otherwise I shall see almost nothing of you, dear heart, and then only at work. There is no reason why you shouldn't go to and fro with me each day, and if I'm called away, you can drive yourself in the Mini. I'll see about getting you replaced at the earliest possible moment, but until we can be married you will stay here under my roof. I have to go to Cologne at the end of next week, but only for two days, and Mama has promised to visit Grandfather at Schuttebeurs, but my aunt will be here. Would you like to telephone your stepmother?'

'Yes, please—but I'm not sure if they're home. I telephoned her nearly a week ago and they were just leaving for Scotland to stay with friends—but only for a week or ten days, I think.' She twiddled the ring on her finger, admiring it. 'I hope it will be convenient— me getting married, I mean.'

The doctor gave her a loving look. 'If it isn't,' he assured her cheerfully, 'we'll get married here. And now, my darling, let us be businesslike for a little while. There are three full clinics tomorrow, aren't there? And you'll be working at each of them. I have patients to see in Zwolle in the evening, but I shall be back about eight o'clock. We'll go out to dinner, somewhere not too far away, if you're not too tired.' He paused: 'That won't do—you will be tired. We will come here and dine alone and if you want to doze off over the coffee you can do so in comfort.'

Philomena giggled. 'Oh, it won't be as bad as all that,' she told him. 'We should be finished soon after seven, you know, and the evening surgery isn't all that busy, but I should like to come here, just with you. Won't it make a lot of extra work, though?'

The doctor looked surprised. 'I imagine not. In fact, everyone is so delighted that we're going to be married that I think it possible that they will enjoy planning our supper.'

'I should have liked a new dress,' observed Philomena. 'You've seen them all now.'

The doctor smiled. 'Yes? I've been wondering how many new outfits I was to be charmed with. I like this one; wear that.'

She looked at him with suspicion. 'I thought you hadn't noticed anything I wore...' She frowned. 'You never looked as though you did.'

'I think that I have noticed everything about you, dearest heart; everything you have said and done and worn.'

She pinkened under his look. 'I should be going back to Mevrouw de Winter's...'

'So you should; I'll take you now and talk to her at

the same time. Could you be packed ready for tomorrow evening, do you think?'

Philomena assured him that she could: 'You're sure that your mother won't mind? Or your aunt?'

He raised his eyebrows. 'My dearest Philly, they will be delighted. And even if they weren't—which is absurd—they are guests in my house.'

Philomena refused to be intimidated by the eyebrows. 'Yes, well—but they're your family.'

'My mother is—Aunt, no—only married into it. She will be leaving soon, anyway.' He shot her a keen glance. 'You don't like her?'

'I don't know her, Walle. I just thought she doesn't like me.'

He said something in Dutch which she took to be the equivalent of nonsense. 'Everyone likes you—how could they do anything else?' He pulled her gently to her feet and kissed her just as gently. 'I'm a very lucky man,' he told her.

He had been right about the clinics. They were full to overflowing; the day flew by with a hurriedly snatched meal at midday with Mevrouw de Winter, aglow with reflected romance, loitering in the doorway, admiring the ring, saying, with the strength of hindsight, that of course anyone could have seen that a wedding was in the offing and what did Miss Parsons intend to wear?

Philomena, her mouth full of her lunch, answered in

her ragged Dutch, assured her landlady that she would tell her in good time, and rushed back to take the baby clinic. It overflowed into the early evening so that she had no time for tea before going over to Doctor de Klein for the evening surgery.

She hadn't seen Walle all day, but she hadn't expected to and in a way she had been glad. It left her free to get on with her work and pack her things with more speed than neatness. All the same, when at last she was free she was both hungry and tired; she wouldn't be a very gay companion that evening, even if she was a happy one. She changed into the green dress and made the most of her face and hair, and arrived downstairs only ten minutes late, to find the doctor sitting in the kitchen, drinking Mevrouw de Winter's excellent coffee while that lady plied him with delighted questions.

The drive to the castle seemed very short and prettier than ever; the June evening sky was clear and unclouded and the country was at its best. The castle gleamed in the late sunshine and Philomena, looking at it with the contented eyes of its prospective mistress, observed: 'It must cost hundreds of pounds to keep in apple pie order.'

'Thousands.' He glanced down at her, smiling. 'Don't worry, Philly, I can afford it.'

She flushed faintly. 'I didn't mean to pry.'

She felt his hand on hers. 'My dear, it is right that you should take an interest in your home; one day soon, when we have the leisure, you shall come into the study and I will explain the upkeep of the castle and tell you about rents and land revenue and everything else you must know. Here we are, and I'm famished!'

Mathias opened the door to them and informed them that Mevrouw van der Tacx had gone to a concert in Zwolle and taken Mevrouw van Niep with her. 'And I have set dinner in the small dining room, *mijnheer*, seeing that it's just the two of you.'

The small dining room wasn't all that small, Philomena discovered. Its circular rosewood table could seat eight very nicely and there was room to spare for the vast sideboard along one wall and the display cabinet between the windows. Its walls were hung with crimson tapestry, almost hidden by the vast number of pictures hung upon it. Nonetheless, it was an elegant room; she could imagine it would be a charming background for a dinner party. Although it was still light, someone had lighted the candles in the great silver candlesticks on the table and there was champagne in its bucket... She had been feeling tired, but now she wasn't any more. Mathias ushered her carefully into her chair and served the soup as though it were a privilege to be in on the party.

They had lobster Thermidor to follow with a salad grown in the kitchen gardens of the castle, then strawberries and cream and water ices, and finally a bowl of fruit from the glasshouses with their coffee.

It was late when they rose from the table; too late to worry about business matters, declared the doctor, time enough for that during the next few days. He took Philomena instead to the small sitting room, where they sat talking until they heard his mother and aunt returning.

Mevrouw van der Tacx swept into the room, very elegant in her evening dress and wrap, to embrace Philomena with a sincere affection which dispelled any doubts she might have about her welcome. Mevrouw van Niep greeted her kindly too, though with reserve, but perhaps she was like that, thought Philomena, listening to Mevrouw van der Tacx's remarks about the concert and music in general. And presently the two ladies went up the stairs to their rooms, leaving Philomena and Walle to sit talking until the night was dark and still.

The days were different now. Philomena still worked, but it wasn't quite the same thing, for Walle drove her in each morning and swept her back for lunch, however hurried, and then fetched her again in the evenings. The clinics were as busy as ever and Philomena, who had supposed that she would find it difficult to work with Walle, discovered that it made no difference at all; at the clinic he was the doctor and she the nurse. He even addressed her as such, turning a bland, serious face to hers, treating her in a polite impersonal manner, and when she taxed him with it, he had laughed and told her that it would be quite impossible in any other way, an opinion to which she had to agree.

And at the castle each evening she spent long hours with him, learning about his home and his family and his work and once or twice meeting his friends and getting to know them too, for they would be her friends now.

With Mevrouw van der Tacx she got on splendidly. 'I always wanted a daughter like you, my dear,' the older lady confided. 'I know that when Walle is married I shan't stay here so frequently, but I hope that you will invite me from time to time and you must certainly come to see me in Friesland. As a family we tend to live far apart, but we are closely knit and like to visit each other!'

Philomena gave her a quick hug. 'You must come as often as you like,' she cried. 'We shall love having you, you must know that. Walle is devoted to you and I have come to love you too.'

And indeed she had, she realised with some astonishment; her stepmother had never aroused such affection as she felt for Walle's mother. It was a pity that she couldn't feel the same for his aunt—that particular aunt, anyway. There had been other aunts and cousins and uncles she had met and liked, but there was something sly about Mevrouw van Niep...

Tritia she saw seldom; she had many friends and was away for days on end, and when she was at the castle they talked trivialities on the rare occasions when they found themselves together. There was so much to do, Philomena discovered; the dogs to walk, Walle to accompany when he went to see a tenant farmer or a sick workman on the estate, and once they visited the woman who had been taken ill in her isolated hut and was now quite recovered and living in the village. Walle was a good landlord as well as a good doctor and he was very rich, she had discovered. It had worried her a little at first; that he had wealth enough to maintain the castle and his comfortable way of life she had accepted, but a visit from the family solicitor so that certain finances might be arranged for her benefit left her surprised; on paper, his income looked enormous, as did the funds from which he drew this income, but as he had pointed out to her in his placid way, the castle needed a good deal of money to maintain and he was fortunate enough to have it. She could only agree with his sensible remark that to allow it to fall into ruins for lack of funds would be a terrible thing to happen. After that she found herself accepting the comfort in which she now lived and as the days went by her happiness was complete, despite the rush and bustle of the clinics, and that wouldn't be for much longer.

She had been at the castle for ten days when Mevrouw van der Tacx went away to visit Walle's grandfather at Schuttebeurs, and two days later Walle went away too, the necessary journey to Cologne to attend a seminar and be the guest of honour at a dinner there, which left Mevrouw van Niep and Philomena to keep each other company.

Walle had wished her goodbye very early in the morning, loath to go and unable not to. 'And when I come back we will fix a day for the wedding,' he told her. 'The new nurse will be coming in a couple of weeks now, the banns have been read, haven't they? There's nothing to stop us marrying when we want to.' He kissed her lingeringly. 'As soon as possible, my dear love.'

Philomena, watching the car going down the drive, thought how very nice it was to be someone's dear love. Two days was a long time, she reflected. She would pass them by making final plans for the wedding. She hadn't decided on the church yet and nor had she bought a dress. She wandered back indoors, her head full of dreams.

CHAPTER NINE

WALLE HAD BEEN GONE for several hours when Philomena got her telephone call. She and Mevrouw van Niep had lunched together, the elder lady reminiscing about the doctor's youth, his brilliant career, his wealth and the glorious times he had had with Tritia. 'Not that I wish to alarm you, my dear,' observed the lady. 'I am quite sure that he has squashed any feelings—any strong feelings—he may have had for her and realised finally that these were not returned. Tritia is such a charming girl and so sought after, it is only natural that she should prefer younger men than Walle.'

To which Philomena had no reply but a murmur which could have meant anything at all. She had accepted the fact the Mevrouw van Niep didn't like her, but she had no need to be nasty about it—and anyway, she told herself, she didn't believe a word of it. Walle would have been a strange man indeed if he hadn't been in love half a dozen times at least, and after all, it was herself he had chosen. She declined her companion's offer of a chat in the sitting room with the excuse that she had a letter to write, and wandered off through the house, looking at its treasures and marvelling that they would soon be hers as well as Walle's.

The telephone call was from her stepmother and she sounded agitated. 'Philly, you simply must come home at once—it's Chloe, she's so ill.'

'What's wrong?' asked Philomena. 'Is she in hospital?'

'Chickenpox, and very badly—the poor darling.' The usually lazy pleasant voice sounded distracted. 'I've a nurse for her—you know how hopeless Miriam and I are at looking after anyone who's ill—but Chloe can't bear her. Darling, you must help—after all, your family comes first.' She added thoughtfully: 'Besides, you're a trained nurse and it's only right that you should look after her.'

Philomena let that pass. 'How long has she been ill?'

'Three days, and she looks terrible and she feels so ill… Could you get a couple of weeks off? I can't remember if you said that you were still working, anyway, I can't see that that matters. Perhaps I should telephone Walle— Oh, Philly, you must come!' The voice was a wail now.

'Walle isn't here, but of course he won't object—I'll catch the first plane I can—is Chloe at home?'

Her stepmother couldn't have heard her, because all

she said was: 'Come straight home, Philly—try and let me know when you will arrive, and I'll meet you.'

'It will be some time tonight at Heathrow, I expect—I'll try and let you know later, and don't worry.'

Philomena put the receiver back and sat quietly for a few minutes, making her plans. Walle wouldn't be back for two days and although she was quite sure that he would telephone, it would be late in the evening; she would be gone long before then. Luckily Mevrouw van Niep was home. She would write Walle a note and ask her to give it to him when he got back and at the same time she would give her a message to pass on when he telephoned. She would have to let Doctor Stanversen and Doctor de Klein know too and get Corrie to take over for a few days. She sighed, wishing that Walle was there to settle everything in a few quiet words, then picked up the telephone once more. Both doctors were out and weren't expected back until late, so all she could do was to leave messages, but Corrie was still at the clinic and cheerfully undertook to see to everything.

'I really ought to see one of the doctors,' explained Philomena worriedly, 'but I just haven't the time to go hunting around for them—besides, no one seems to know just where they are. If I'm quick I can get a plane from Schiphol, Mathias will drive me there, it's only just two o'clock and I can be away from here in half an hour.' She was thinking out loud now. 'It's two hours to Schiphol, give or take half an hour, that makes it about five o'clock, and I might be lucky and get on the next flight—I can be at Heathrow by the evening... Corrie, you will explain, won't you?'

Reassured by Corrie's friendly voice, she went in search of Mevrouw van Niep, sitting in her stately fashion in the small sitting room, her embroidery frame before her. She looked up as Philomena went in and although she smiled her pale eyes were cold. She listened in silence to what Philomena had to tell her and at the end inclined her head graciously.

'You have done quite rightly, Philomena. I shall certainly give Walle your message when he telephones—so much better than a note, don't you think?'

'I'd be very grateful—if you could explain and tell him that I'm sorry I had to go like this without warning. I know he'll understand; my stepmother seemed very upset and she's not a very practical person. I've left messages for Doctor Stanversen and Doctor de Klein, and Corrie has promised to do my work. Do you suppose someone could drive me to Schiphol? I can be ready in ten minutes or so.'

Mevrouw van Niep gave her a thoughtful look and took so long to reply that Philomena was about to repeat her request when she answered with a little rush: 'Certainly, Philomena, I'll see to it at once. Have you enough money with you? Is there anything you might require?'

Philomena gave her a grateful glance. 'You're very

kind, but I have everything I need.' She spoke with more warmth than usual; she had misjudged Mevrouw van Niep, who was being very kind and helpful, and over her swift packing, she reflected that it was fortunate that Mevrouw van Niep would be there to speak to Walle when he telephoned. So much better than leaving a message with one of the servants; Mevrouw van Niep would be able to explain and it wouldn't sound so bad.

All the same, she worried a little as she sat in the plane, halfway to England and with the leisure now to wonder if she had done the right thing. Perhaps she should have waited and talked to Walle herself but then it would have meant waiting until the morning to start her journey, and supposing something prevented him from telephoning after all. She comforted herself with the thought that his aunt would explain, and she would be back in a few days, she reminded herself, watching the first English fields slip past below, peaceful in the evening light. If Chloe was really ill, she would have to go to hospital, and if it was just chickenpox she would recover quickly. She had found time to telephone from Schiphol and Molly had answered; her stepmother was out, but Molly was sure she would drive up to Heathrow and fetch Philomena.

She had to wait at the airport, but she hadn't expected anyone to be waiting for her; she whiled away the time with a cup of coffee while she caught up with the news, and she was just beginning to feel a little uneasy when she saw her stepmother at the barrier.

Mrs Parsons looked harassed and upset, and after a brief greeting, the answers she gave to Philomena's questions were vague and not very much to the point. That Chloe was covered in spots and had lost her looks was made abundantly clear, but everything else was shrugged off with a quick: 'Well, how should I know, Philly, I'm not a nurse.' She smiled apologetically. 'Shall we talk about something cheerful? I'm so tired… Have you made plans for your wedding? A quiet one, I gather. Very wise, darling—you know how much I have your interest at heart and you'd not stand a chance if you had a big wedding—I mean, everyone would be looking at Chloe and Miriam, wouldn't they, when they should be looking at you?' She gave a little laugh. 'That would never do, a wedding is supposed to be a bride's day. No, you're quite right, darling, a nice quiet ceremony—there are plenty of village churches near home. We can shop around for a pretty outfit. I suppose you'll be going straight back to Holland?'

'I expect so,' Philomena agreed quietly. Her stepmother wasn't being deliberately unkind, but her words had hurt more than she could have believed possible; her own reasons for a quiet wedding had been the very ones her stepmother had voiced, but there had been no need to put them into words. She drew a calming breath. 'Poor Chloe, I'm sorry she's so ill, but it shouldn't last long—once the fever's gone she'll be quite all right except for the rash, and that will die down soon.'

'That horrid rash, and just as the Pierce boy was on the point of proposing. Heaven knows, Chloe has had to work hard enough…'

'I shouldn't have thought she would have needed to lift so much as a finger,' Philomena observed.

'Well, she did,' snapped Mrs Parsons, 'and now it's probably all for nothing.'

'But if he loves her he won't care a fig for a few spots.'

Her stepmother clashed the gears. 'That's what you think,' she snapped. 'Just wait until that Walle of yours sees you without any make-up!'

Philomena was on the point of saying that he had, frequently, and it hadn't made any difference to his feelings as far as she could tell. Instead she said soothingly: 'Let's stop at that all-night place along here and have some coffee and then I'll drive the rest of the way, you must be tired out.'

Her stepmother dozed after that, but when they reached Wareham at last she sat up quickly and said urgently: 'Don't go home, Philly, take the Weymouth road.'

Philomena slowed the car. 'But why aren't we going home?'

'Chloe isn't there—I'll explain. You remember that cottage Molly's aunt used to live in at Osmington? She rents it out in the summer now—well, Chloe's there— there's someone with her, a girl who's done some nursing. She lives in Wareham, and she said she'd stay until you got there.'

'But why?' Philomena was as puzzled as she sounded.

Her stepmother answered impatiently: 'The rash, of course—darling Chloe had to go away. Supposing someone saw the poor sweet? She'd never want to show her face again.'

'I don't see why not—rashes fade, there's no reason why she should have any scars, unless she scratches.'

Her companion shuddered, genuinely horrified at the idea. 'You must see…'

Philomena saw only too well: she had been called home, not because Chloe was really ill, but because the girl was too vain of her appearance to be nursed like anyone else. Fine friends she's got, thought Philomena, if they can't bear the sight of a few spots! Presumably Chloe intended to stay at the cottage until she was her own lovely self once more, and Philly, so conveniently a nurse, should be the one to stay with her. She felt tears prick her eyelids. She need not have come, there was nothing urgent about Chloe's illness; she could have been with Walle.

The cottage was on the edge of the small village, not exactly isolated but standing well apart from a scattering of similar dwellings. It was screened from the lane by overgrown hedges and trees and the path to its small front door was overgrown with roses and weeds and brambles. Philomena parked the car and got out, glad to see that despite the lateness of the hour there was a light in one of the downstairs windows. The front door was opened as she and her stepmother reached it, and a young woman, dressed in a light coat, ushered them inside without a word and before either of them could speak she broke the silence. 'You're late—if this is the lady who's going to stay, I'm ready to leave now, Mrs Parsons. Your daughter doesn't need the two of us. There's no reason why she shouldn't be at home like anyone else, you know—she's not feverish any more, and you told me the doctor said she'd be over it in no time at all.' She gave Mrs Parsons a hard stare. 'A lot of nonsense,' she finished.

'Out of the question,' Mrs Parsons spoke sharply, 'but come back with me if you wish to. My daughter will look after her sister. Just tell her anything she needs to know and we'll go.' She turned to a silent Philomena. 'You'll manage, won't you, darling? The doctor said a week or ten days before the rash goes, and that was four days ago. There's no telephone, but I'll come and see how you're getting on in a few days.'

Philomena was almost too furious to speak. Her stepmother's colossal selfishness in bringing her all the way from Holland just to be with Chloe, who wasn't even ill, had left her too indignant for words. She said now in a cold voice: 'A few days won't do, will you come tomorrow? I should like to talk to you.' She would have liked to have said a good deal more, but the young

woman was standing with them and showed no signs
of leaving them alone; perhaps she was afraid that Mrs
Parsons would go without her.

Mrs Parsons looked surprised and then annoyed.

'Tomorrow will be awkward; there's a bridge party,
besides...'

'Then you'll have to cancel it,' said Philomena. 'I'll
expect you after lunch.'

She got a grudging nod in reply and: 'I don't know
what's come over you, Philly.'

The young woman was getting impatient; she fired
off what information she thought necessary about the
patient, the provisions in the cottage and where the
clean linen was kept. 'And I didn't make up the bed,'
she went on. 'Why should I? No one made it up for me.'

A difficult remark to answer. Philomena held the
door open a little wider and watched the two of them
go down the path. Neither of them looked back.

Chloe, when she went to look, was asleep and not
looking in the least ill—indeed, there were few pock-
marks to be seen on her face, certainly she wasn't the
hideous sight Philomena had been led to believe. She
closed the door of the small room and went to look at
the other room across the landing. The tumbled bed
was uninviting and at the sight of it Philomena realised
how tired she was. All the same, something had to be
done about it. She made it up with fresh linen, carried
up her case, went down again to the dark little kitchen

at the back of the cottage and made herself a cup of tea, and then went to bed. Perhaps, she told herself bracingly, things wouldn't look quite so beastly in the morning. If only Walle had been there; calm and placid and knowing just what to do.

Walle, at that late hour, was neither calm nor placid, although he knew exactly what to do. No one at the medical school dinner he had attended that evening had known that he was in a towering rage; a little distrait, perhaps, but then, they told each other, these clever men so often were. He had telephoned earlier that evening and when his aunt had told him that Philomena wasn't there, he had only been momentarily put out. It was when Mevrouw van Niep had added with something like relish: 'She's gone home, Walle—to England,' that he had felt a flicker of unease.

His silence had disconcerted her and she had made haste to add: 'We had a long talk this morning. She's been unhappy, Walle—I don't think you knew that, did you? She realised that you could never be happy together. She wanted to make a clean break.'

Walle's voice had been very quiet. 'She left a letter for me?'

'Well, no, dear. She asked me to say what I have just told you, although she did say that she would write to you and she said particularly that you were not to telephone until you had heard from her. She left this afternoon.' She added with some anxiety: 'You're not coming home?'

'No, Aunt, that's impossible. I shall be back tomorrow evening.'

Mevrouw van Niep let out a sigh of relief. 'I thought that, Walle. I shall be here and so will Tritia. Your mother won't be back for several days, though.' She added: 'I'm sorry, Walle, Philomena was a charming girl but not for you.'

'No?' Something in his voice uttering the single word made her frown, although it turned to a smile as he added: 'But Tritia is, perhaps?'

She agreed too eagerly. 'Something I have always longed for, Walle.'

'I'm flattered that you have my interest at heart, Aunt.' He wished her goodbye with his usual calm and she, well satisfied with her meddling, sat down to contemplate a future in which dear Tritia would become the mistress of the castle and she herself living there in luxury and ease, for of course the dear girl would be grateful.

The doctor arrived back before he was expected, although in a household as well ordered as his, this made no difference. Mathias met him at the door with his usual stately welcome, relieved him of his overnight bag, assured him that dinner would be advanced to whatever hour he wished and opened his study door invitingly, but the doctor responded to these courtesies in an absent-minded fashion and beyond asking if there had been any news of Miss Parsons, had nothing to say. 'Where's my aunt?' he enquired at length.

'In the small sitting room, *mijnheer*—Mevrouw van der Tacx has returned unexpectedly and is with her.'

The doctor nodded. 'Thanks. Pack me a bag, will you? I shall be leaving for England first thing in the morning.' He glanced at the old man and saw the look of pleased satisfaction on his face. 'I shall be bringing Miss Parsons back with me—see to her room, will you?' He added quietly: 'We need her back, don't we, Mathias?'

His faithful servant nodded a delighted head. 'Oh, yes indeed! We none of us could understand...'

'I'm a bit vague about it myself,' remarked the doctor over his shoulder, and went into the sitting room.

His greeting was affable to the two ladies sitting there. As he kissed his mother he said pleasantly: 'Good of you to come at once, Mama.' They smiled at each other before he turned to his aunt.

'Shall we make it brief?' he wanted to know, silkily pleasant still. 'I telephoned Philomena's home within minutes of your message, Aunt, and had an entirely different story from the one which you told me—now I wonder why you should wish to mislead me so grossly? Philomena went home because one of her stepsisters is ill and I feel sure that the message she asked you to deliver wasn't at all the one which you gave. I cannot see why you should have wished to change it. You must have known that it would have caused doubt and anxiety—or perhaps that was what you wanted?'

His voice had become very soft and there was a small smile around his mouth. Both ladies stirred in their chairs; the doctor was in a rage, and his mother at least hoped that he would hold it in check.

He did. Presently he went on hurriedly: 'You must think me a great fool, Aunt; I cannot conceive of any man neglecting to take immediate steps to discover the whereabouts of the girl he intends to marry—you shouldn't have advised me so strongly not to telephone, you know, you were too eager.'

His blue eyes were like ice. 'Perhaps it would be as well if you were to leave my house—after dinner, of course. One of the maids shall pack for you. I have already telephoned Tritia and her things will be sent on. It may interest you to know that I have never felt the faintest desire to marry the girl...'

Mevrouw van Niep interrupted him shrilly. 'She adores you, she wants to go everywhere with you...'

The doctor made a furious sound, half snort half groan. 'My dear aunt, she regards me as an elderly type, useful upon which to practise her wiles when there is no one else handy. In time she will find someone of her own age and settle down, without any help from you, I fancy.' He added blightingly: 'You have meddled too much.'

He walked over to the sofa table. 'And now what about a drink before dinner?'

It was a good deal later, after Mevrouw van Niep had left, that he asked his mother: 'You didn't mind coming back at a moment's notice? You will be here when we get back?'

She smiled at him. 'Of course I'll be here, Walle. I have been very much shocked by your aunt's extraordinary behaviour. Thank heaven you made enquiries at once—poor Philomena, having to rush off like that! I hope that her stepsister isn't very ill.'

Her son gave her a thoughtful look. 'Somehow I doubt it, but we will know soon enough. I'm leaving very early, Mama, I should be in Wareham by late afternoon, perhaps sooner.'

'Philly knows that you are coming? You left a message?'

He smiled. 'No—I shall deliver my own message, my dear.'

Philomena was tired. She had spent an exhausting day reassuring Chloe that she wouldn't be disfigured for life, dabbing lotion on spots and coaxing her to eat the meals she had cooked with some difficulty on the small electric stove the cottage boasted. Now she had coaxed her back into her bed, given her her supper and had left her with a pile of magazines while she went downstairs to get a meal for herself. Twice during the day she had essayed to leave Chloe, walk through the village to the main road where there was a telephone box, and telephone Walle, but her stepsister became almost hysterical at the very idea of being left even for an hour and Philomena had to give up the idea. She hurried over a boiled egg and toast and started on a letter. The milkman could take it for her in the morning and even though it would take several days it was better than nothing. Her stepmother hadn't come; probably she had never intended to in the first place, and Philomena had never felt so cut off and helpless. The idea that she might hire a car somewhere and take Chloe home and then return to Holland had crossed her mind, but then supposing her stepsister should take cold or become ill, the blame would be hers entirely.

It was very quiet, the evening sky still light and the air warm. Somewhere inside the cottage walls a mouse nibbled and scratched, and the small sound made the quiet even quieter. Philomena wrote on, page after page, pouring out her indignation and worry. It was deep dusk by the time she had finished, and when she should have gone to bed, Chloe demanded that her rash must be treated before she could settle for the night. It was late by the time Philomena put out her light for the last time, so that she overslept and missed the milkman who would have taken her letter. There was no post either; she had half expected something from her stepmother and, although she knew it was quite impossible, she had hoped for a letter from Walle, which was silly, since he didn't even know where she was, she supposed. She dressed herself rather grumpily and set about ordering their day.

Chloe was better. She looked a fright, true enough, but the rash would fade in time and there was nothing wrong with the girl other than a peevishness hard to put up with and a ridiculous fear that someone would see her before she was restored to her usual good looks. She spent the day in the small overcrowded sitting room, worrying about her looks and screaming and crying in the most alarming fashion whenever Philomena suggested that she could be left alone for a short time while she walked to the telephone.

She gave up in the end and went into the kitchen to make their tea, and while the kettle boiled wandered down the short path outside the back door and peered into the lane. It wound away to open country on one side and on the other began the slow climb to the village and the main road. There was a car coming down the hill; she couldn't see it, but she could hear it. It came into view a second later—her stepmother. Philomena, forgetful of the kettle, went right into the lane and saw that there was another car too—the Khamsin, with Walle at the wheel. Mrs Parsons slid to an untidy stop and called something, but Philomena didn't hear her. She had sped past her and come to a halt beside the Khamsin. She didn't know that tears were running down her cheeks and even if she did, she wouldn't have cared.

For a man as large as he was, the doctor had got out

of the car very fast indeed. Philomena ran into his arms and stayed there, muttering and mumbling away in a happy voice into his shoulder, and he let her be just for a few moments. Presently she raised a streaky face to look at him and laughed a little.

'I always seem to be howling,' she told him, 'only I'm so happy—I didn't know what to do and there was no telephone and I didn't think you'd know where I was—I left a message…' She stopped because he was kissing her, but presently she went on: 'I wrote you a letter, but I missed the milkman… Walle, did you ever want to marry Tritia? Your aunt…'

The doctor regarded her tear-stained face lovingly. 'No, my dearest darling, I never wanted to marry anyone, only you. My aunt is prone to exaggerate and she is forgetful.'

'Oh—did she forget my message?'

'Shall we say that she got it a little muddled, but that doesn't matter now. I've come to take you home, Philly—and before you say another word I have—er—persuaded your stepmother to take Chloe back with her. This ridiculous obsession about her looks won't do her any good at all, as I have explained. If she must keep to her room she can do so in her own home.'

Philomena's grip on his sleeve tightened. 'Walle, I knew you'd arrange everything. Can we go now?'

'No, my love. Your mother and Chloe are going at once, you and I will follow later. It seems a good opportunity to make our plans for the future.'

Philomena would have agreed to anything. She said meekly: 'Yes, Walle,' and then: 'My stepmother's calling—I should go in...'

'For the last time, my darling, but after this you will be at no one's beck and call.' He tucked an arm in hers. 'We'll go together.'

It wasn't all that easy getting the two of them away. Chloe, still very much wrapped up in her appearance, was disposed to sulk and might have gone on for hours if the doctor had not pointed out that tears and futile rage would inevitably prolong the rash and that if she intended being a bridesmaid at Philomena's wedding, then she had better start from that very moment to cheer up.

'Bridesmaid?' asked Philomena, frowning a little.

Her future husband turned a placid face towards her. 'My love, would you be very vexed if we had a really big wedding? Of course, if you say so, we will have the quietest ceremony possible, but I have so many friends and such a large family, and they'll all wish to be present.' He contrived to look hopeful and a little apprehensive at the same time, and Philomena said at once: 'Then we'll have a big wedding—where?'

'At home,' interpolated Mrs Parsons. 'Walle did just mention it to me when he arrived, that was if you agreed.' She added rather crossly, 'I'm sure you know your own minds best.'

'Oh, indeed we do,' agreed Walle blandly. 'Should

you not be going? We will follow very shortly—we'll dine on the way. I don't know if Philly has a key?'

'Yes, I have, we can let ourselves in.' Philomena couldn't keep the happiness out of her voice. Her 'They've gone', an obvious remark, was nevertheless uttered with profound satisfaction. 'What plans?' she wanted to know.

The doctor looked vague. 'Plans? Oh, this and that, my dearest girl. Shall we sit for a little while and talk? It seems a long time since I've seen you.' He stared round the sitting room, studying the furniture with distaste. 'The sofa, I think.'

Philomena, curled up close to him, heaved a sigh of content and then said: 'Why do you want a big wedding? I mean, are all your relations coming?'

'Yes, they are, and as many friends as we can get into the church. My darling Philly, I want the whole world to be there to share our day and our happiness. You will wear white, my love, and you will be beautiful, as beautiful as you are now.'

'That's the nicest bit of nonsense I've heard for a long time. Walle, is your mother at the castle?' She thought a moment. 'And your aunt and Tritia?'

'My mother, yes. My aunt and Tritia left yesterday.' Something in his voice warned her not to pursue the matter further.

He wasn't going to tell her; something had happened while she was away. She discovered that she didn't care in the least.

* * *

Philomena twitched a fold of creamy white chiffon away from Uncle Ben's foot and contemplated her bouquet— roses of the same creamy white tipped with pink. There was orange blossom too, and orchids and stephanotis. She touched a rose petal just to reassure herself that it was real, for until that moment the morning had been a dream, and even now with Uncle Ben sitting beside her in the white ribboned limousine, she still didn't quite believe that she was getting married to Walle. A thousand doubts filled her head. She was quite unsuited to become the mistress of a rich man's castle, she was plain and quite uninteresting; Walle had made a mistake and probably he was regretting it at this very moment, only of course he would be too kind to do anything about it... She closed her eyes at the horrid thought, remembering what her stepmother had said only an hour or so ago when she had visited her in her bedroom to approve her appearance.

'You're a lucky girl, Philly,' she had observed. 'You're not pretty, my dear, and you haven't much money—not that that matters; Walle has enough for a dozen—and you're not a girl to attract men, are you? And yet here you are, marrying one of the wealthiest and handsomest men I've ever laid eyes on.' She had laughed quite kindly, not seeing Philomena's wince. 'We'll have to call it Philomena's Miracle, won't we?'

Uncle Ben eased himself upright. 'Here we are, Philly. Ready to face the crowd?'

It surprised her to see so many people waiting outside the church, but somehow they seemed part and parcel of her unreal world. She gained the porch and was struck by the loveliness of her stepsisters; in pink chiffon and floppy-brimmed straw hats wreathed with roses, they looked superb, and she told them so while they fussed with her train and veil, assuring her with facile good nature that she looked marvellous.

She smiled at them from a face made pale by her doubts, and took Uncle Ben's arm.

The aisle looked unending, the church crowded with a sea of faces turned over elegant shoulders; her stepmother had done exactly what Walle had wished— asked every friend and acquaintance to the wedding. Philomena could see him standing at the end of the aisle, his broad back impeccable in a grey morning coat; he was the only one in the whole church who wasn't looking at her. They were a third of the way now and she faltered for a moment, and at the same moment he turned very deliberately, and at the sight of his kind, loving face all her doubts vanished as though they had never been. A faint lovely pink washed her pale cheeks and her green eyes began to sparkle. She was the most beautiful girl in the world and he loved her; his look told her that as plainly as though he had shouted it the length of the church.

She lifted her chin a little and the beginnings of a smile curved her mouth. The unreal future was real after all; it was theirs, hers and Walle's, to share. She wanted to run the rest of the way and tell him so, and as usual he read her thoughts. His face remained grave, but she was near enough to see the sparks of laughter in his eyes.

Welcome to cowboy country...

Turn the page for a sneak preview of
TEXAS BABY
by
Kathleen O'Brien
An exciting new title from Harlequin Superromance
for everyone
who loves stories about the West.

Harlequin Superromance—
Where life and love weave together in emotional and
unforgettable ways.

CHAPTER ONE

CHASE TRANSFERRED his gaze to the road and identified a foreign spot on the horizon. A car. Almost half a mile away, where the straight, tree-lined drive met the public road. He could tell it was coming too fast, but judging the speed of a vehicle moving straight toward you was tricky.

It wasn't until it was about two hundred yards away that he realized the driver must be drunk…or crazy. Or both.

The guy was going maybe sixty. On a private drive, out here in ranch country, where kids or horses or tractors or stupid chickens might come darting out any minute, that was criminal. Chase straightened from his comfortable slouch and waved his hands.

"Slow down, you fool," he called out. He took the porch steps quickly and began walking fast down the driveway.

The car veered oddly, from one lane to another, then up onto the slight rise of the thick green spring grass. It just barely missed the fence.

"Slow down, damn it!"

He couldn't see the driver, and he didn't recognize this automobile. It was small and old, and couldn't have cost much even when it was new. It was probably white, but now it needed either a wash or a new paint job or both.

"Damn it, what's wrong with you?"

At the last minute, he had to jump away, because the idiot behind the wheel clearly wasn't going to turn to avoid a collision. He couldn't believe it. The car kept coming, finally slowing a little, but it was too late.

Still going about thirty miles an hour, it slammed into the large, white-brick pillar that marked the front boundaries of the house. The pillar wasn't going to give an inch, so the car had to. The front end folded up like a paper fan.

It seemed to take forever for the car to settle, as if the trauma happened in slow motion, reverberating from the front to the back of the car in ripples of destruction. The front windshield suddenly seemed to ice over with lethal bits of glassy frost. Then the side windows exploded.

The front driver's door wrenched open, as if the car wanted to expel its contents. Metal buckled hideously. Small pieces, like hubcaps and mirrors, skipped and ricocheted insanely across the oyster-shell driveway.

Finally, everything was still. Into the silence, a plume of steam shot up like a geyser, smelling of rust and heat. Its snakelike hiss almost smothered the low, agonized moan of the driver.

Chase's anger had disappeared. He didn't feel anything but a dull sense of disbelief. Things like this didn't happen in real life. Not in his life. Maybe the sun had actually put him to sleep....

But he was already kneeling beside the car. The driver was a woman. The frosty glass-ice of the windshield was dotted with small flecks of blood. She must have hit it with her head, because just below her hairline a red liquid was seeping out. He touched it. He tried to wipe it away before it reached her eyebrow, though, of course that made no sense at all. Her eyes were shut.

Was she conscious? Did he dare move her? Her dress was covered in glass, and the metal of the car was sticking out lethally in all the wrong places.

Then he remembered, with an intense relief, that every good medical man in the county was here, just behind the house, drinking his champagne. He found his phone and paged Trent.

The woman moaned again.

Alive, then. Thank God for that.

He saw Trent coming toward him, starting out at a lope, but quickly switching to a full run.

"Get Dr. Marchant," Chase called. "Don't bother with 911."

Trent didn't take long to assess the situation. A fraction of a second, and he began pulling out his cell phone and running toward the house.

The yelling seemed to have roused the woman. She

opened her eyes. They were blue and clouded with pain and confusion.

"Chase," she said.

His breath stalled. His head pulled back. "What?"

Her only answer was another moan, and he wondered if he had imagined the word. He reached around her and put his arm behind her shoulders. She was tiny. Probably petite by nature, but surely way too thin. He could feel her shoulder blades pushing against her skin, as fragile as the wishbone in a turkey.

She seemed to have passed out, so he put his other arm under her knees and lifted her out. He tried to avoid the jagged metal, but her skirt caught on a piece and the tearing sound seemed to wake her again.

"No," she said. "Please."

"I'm just trying to help," he said. "It's going to be all right."

She seemed profoundly distressed. She wriggled in his arms, and she was so weak, like a broken bird. It made him feel too big and brutish. And intrusive. As if touching her this way, his bare hands against the warm skin behind her knees, were somehow a transgression.

He wished he could be more delicate. But he smelled gasoline, and he knew it wasn't safe to leave her here.

Finally he heard the sound of voices, as guests began to run around the side of the house, alerted by Trent. Dr. Marchant was at the front, racing toward them as if he were forty instead of seventy. Susannah was right behind him, her green dress floating around her trim legs.

"Please," the woman in his arms murmured again. She looked at him, the expression in her blue eyes lost and bewildered. He wondered if she might be on drugs. Hitting her head on the windshield might account for this unfocused, glazed look, but it couldn't explain the crazy driving.

"Please, put me down. Susannah… The wedding…"

Chase's arms tightened instinctively, and he froze in his tracks. She whimpered, and he realized he might be hurting her. "Say that again?"

"The wedding. I have to stop it."

* * * * *

Be sure to look for TEXAS BABY,
available September 11, 2007,
as well as other fantastic Superromance titles
available in September.

HARLEQUIN®

Mediterranean NIGHTS™

*Experience glamour, elegance, mystery and revenge
aboard the high seas....*

Coming in September 2007...

BREAKING ALL
THE RULES

by

Marisa Carroll

Aboard the cruise ship *Alexandra's Dream* for
some R & R, sports journalist Lola Sandler is
surprised to spot pro-golfer Eric Lashman.
Years after walking away from the pro circuit
with no explanation to the public, Eric now
finds himself teaching aboard a cruise ship.

Lola smells a career-making exposé...
but their developing relationship may
force her to make a difficult choice.

www.eHarlequin.com

HM38963

REQUEST YOUR FREE BOOKS!
2 FREE NOVELS PLUS 2
FREE GIFTS!

From the Heart, For the Heart

ATHENA FORCE

Heart-pounding romance and thrilling adventure.

Professional negotiator Lindsey Novak is faced with her biggest challenge—to buy back Teal Arnett, a young woman with unique powers. In the process Lindsey uncovers a devastating plot that involves scientists from around the globe, and all of them lead to one woman who is bent on destroying Athena Academy...at any cost.

LOOK FOR

THE GOOD THIEF

by Judith Leon

Available September wherever you buy books.

AF38973

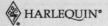

EVERLASTING LOVE™

Every great love has a story to tell™

Third time's a charm.

Texas summers. Charlie Morrison.
Jasmine Boudreaux has always connected
the two. Her relationship with Charlie
begins and ends in high school. Twenty
years later it begins again—and ends again.
Now fate has stepped in one more time—
will Jazzy and Charlie finally give in to
the love they've shared all this time?

Look for

Summer After Summer
by
Ann DeFee

**Available September
wherever books are sold.**